EMMA GLASS was born in Wales in 1987 and is now based in London, where she writes and works as a children's nurse. Her debut novel *Peach* was published by Bloomsbury in 2018, has been translated into seven languages and was long listed for the International Dylan Thomas Prize.

@Emmas_Window

D1346916

rest and be thankful

emma glass

BLOOMSBURY PUBLISHING
LONDON · OXFORD · NEW YORK · NEW DELHI · SYDNEY

BLOOMSBURY PUBLISHING
Bloomsbury Publishing Plc
50 Bedford Square, London, WC1B 3DP, UK
29 Earlsfort Terrace, Dublin 2, Ireland

BLOOMSBURY, BLOOMSBURY PUBLISHING and the Diana logo are
trademarks of Bloomsbury Publishing Plc

First published in Great Britain 2020
Copyright © Emma Glass, 2021

A catalogue record for this book is available from the British Library

ISBN: PB: 978-1-5266-0922-9; EBOOK: 978-1-5266-0109-4

2 4 6 8 10 9 7 5 3 1

Typeset by Integra Software Services Pvt. Ltd.
Printed and bound in Great Britain by CPI Group (UK) Ltd, Croydon CR0 4YY

To find out more about our authors and books visit www.bloomsbury.com
and sign up for our newsletters

For nurses

Where You End, I Begin

The door is swinging, heavy, thumping against the wall. Each thump marks a person entering, marks a person exiting, marks the solid purposeful movements of the people in the room. Marks our collective breath in, breath out, we breathe together. Held too long. We hold and wait for the beat to return. The door thumps against the wall too hard this time, someone looks up and says no no, there are too many people in here now, please go. The ones that are left look around the room at each other. We all have the same eyes, the same chapped lips and wet brows. We are all different shades of blue.

The door is closed but the thumping continues, a steady dull pumping sound, and every now and then a puff of air a puff of air and the thumping continues. The sound is hollow. The sound is bone pounding on soft bone, a flat heart, lungs filled with oxygen from a tank, oxygen soon to spill and fill the belly and the pumping will be harder and my arms are aching already. My feet are off the floor,

I am kneeling next to the little one. I am over her body with my weight. I am the thumping sound. My fingers are interlocked, the heel of my hand is red and sore, my hands and arms are drained white, two long fixed posts pounding. I am counting. Am I counting out loud or am I counting in my head? I feel the bed creak as more weight is added. Someone is moving close to me with a tray of needles, I see the corners of white paper towels unfolding, draping over the little legs. I move my eyes off the chest, there are faces all around me, distorted, crooked with concentration. These are the faces of people I don't know very well, but they are the faces of people I trust.

There are tools everywhere. Tools for fixing the broken. I think of my father with his toolbox rattling. Opening, nails and screws rolling across the workbench. A wrench for this. A screwdriver. Holding still. And then the all-important squirt of oil. We must oil it or it will squeak and stick. He reaches up for a rag hanging on a metal hook and wipes his big hands, brown from working outside, cracked and dry from endless wet weather. I marvel at the big blue bulging veins. We could do with one of those now. A big vein. Or we will have to drill into bone to get fluid inside. Hands run up the limp limbs. There is nothing here, there is nothing here. There is nothing on the other side. The hands travel down the legs. They examine the feet but the feet are cold.

The veins are thin and buried deep in the cold, like saplings under snow.

I close my eyes to drown out the sound of the drill. The leg vibrates as the needle goes in and then it pops and then it stops. I hear someone say 'Jesus' and I wonder if it was me.

Lines are connected. Fluid is injected. I am told by the nurse in the darkest blue to keep going, to keep pace. Time stretches, rolling out clumsily like cling film, air holes, splits, wrinkles. We will be told of the smooth, controlled management of the situation. But I will remember the breaths missed, the shaking hands, the wrong-size tube, the dropped vials, the spilt fluid, the people, all the people aimlessly standing and staring and shitting themselves.

I turn my head to the window and see her mother. She has one hand covering her eyes, no, not covering, clawing at her eyes, one arm pressed against the glass. She is bent in half, barely standing. A nurse is behind her, one hand on her shoulder, another arm ready to catch her. A position we have all been taught. We are all taught to brace. I look back down at my threaded fingers. Locked in. Pain rages up my arms and across my shoulders. I keep going. Each compression means everything.

And this could all mean nothing.

The darkest blue asks me to pause. The world stops. I watch her face as she comes close to me, she reaches for the little arm, she presses deeply for a pulse. The determination on her face is years deep, cracked like unloved concrete. She steps back and nods, she touches my aching shoulder and says, 'You'll sleep well tonight.'

I Dream of Darkness

The ceiling is collapsing. Shards of plaster strike the bed. Chipped paint flakes and falls. Falls like snow-flakes. Snow and cold. Coldness and wetness, but no water. Through the small hole, through the slits and cracks, I see stars.

I push through the rubble and crumble of ceiling and stretch my arms to the sky, reach up and rip the hole wide open. Reaching, I realise I can touch the sky. I float through the ceiling and I am close. Endless night. Deep blue. Colder as I float closer. Ice runs through my airways, my breath is a silver cloud. I press my palms against the surface and feel the coldness of the night. It sticks deep in my bones. Brittle ice, bitter cold. My shuddering skeleton rattles against the thick sheet of frozen sky. Dense and dark. The stars have disappeared.

I push against the solid sky to propel myself away from the impenetrable cold. My hands are blue and numb. I think I might fall. The cold has turned my core to concrete, I think I will drop like a stone, but I sink slowly, slowly down. The sky spreads out beneath me and is all around. Thick midnight ink. Sinking slowly. Thick ink but then thinner and thin and then I realise I can swim. I swim strangely through the deep blue, my arms and legs convulsing until the ice melts away from my muscles.

I swim through different shades of dark. Blue, black, dark blue, darker black. I follow the little specks of light that fleck from the glittering frost forming on my fingertips. The moon shines somewhere. I feel water ripple between my fingers as I move forwards. Cold water surrounds me. I'm in a lake. The lake has frozen over. I am trapped in darkness, treading the bitter water. I have been swimming forever. Tiredness tries to take me down to the bottom of the lake, to lie down and sleep on the soft bed of silken black reeds. They billow beautifully, dancing with the gentle current. My heavy eyelids weigh me down as I drift closer to the darkness. To sleep, just for a moment, to rest. My limbs are seized by cold and fatigue. I drift closer down to the reed bed, steady as a plank, ready to close my eyes and sleep the rest of my life, the soft sounds of the rippling reeds and water swooshing, soothing me to peaceful sleep. Then, I see.

At first, a figure, a faceless form, a shadow settled in silt. Reeds have grown over, woven and bound the body. A body. Draped in black, a black dress swelling, skirts surging. As I drift closer, I see her face, her features drawn and shaded softly in graphite pencil, smudged across her papery skin. Close, almost close enough to touch her. I lift my arm of lead and frost-bound fingers to touch her luminous cheek.

Her eyes flick open. The hushing gushing sounds of the sucking water stop. All noise and colour drain away. In the pitch black her face shines sickly white, picked out by a shard of moonlight. She slowly opens her mouth, a black hole, wide.

'WAKE UP.'

The words gurgle loudly from her mouth, her mouth opens wider and wider until her jaw falls away, her face falls away, blackness remains. Her words rise in silver bubbles. I look down into the darkness as the reeds reach out to tangle around my toes and tug me down into nothingness. I kick and flail with dead-weight limbs through the freezing water, trying to propel myself to the surface, her words making waves, rushing behind me through the water, lifting me up.

My head hits the ice. I slam my fists against it until my skin is bruised and bleeding. I taste metal in my mouth. There is no shift or drift in the ice. It caps the lake tightly. No air. No breathing. Screaming, until my lungs lock and stop. I don't want to die in the dark. Don't want to drown. What happens if you die in a dream? The water in my lungs weighs me down. Nothing in me but cold water and darkness. Nothing to fight with, nothing to fight for. All lights out. Just hush and shushing water. Soothing. And soon to be silent. A soft way to end.

I'm Underwater Again

'WAKE UP.'

You shake me gently but I am shocked by the sound of your voice close to my waterlogged ear and I hit my head against the wooden headboard. I am awake.

You ask me if I'm okay, you touch my head, trying to be tender but the strokes of your dry fingers drag my hair back. Hairs pull from the roots of my scalp, the sharp pain cuts through me like chalk screeching, sketching on a blackboard. My teeth grit. You take your hand away and wipe it on the quilt cover. Your mouth turns down in disgust. You tell me I am soaking wet, I am late for work, you spit the words. You remain disgusted and get out of bed. I touch my head and feel the sore spot spreading like spilt milk under my fingertips. I try to open my eyes fully and clear the blear, but the sleep has stuck fast. I rub the crusts from the corners and lose some lashes. Bright light pries my eyes open and burns away the darkness of my dream. The ice has melted and left me soaking wet, my skin is drenched, the bed sheets are saturated with sweat. I roll on to my stomach and push my face into the wet pillow. It smells like pond water. I breathe deeply in the dampness and then I cough and then I splutter. My lungs are tight and tired. Everything aches. I feel weighed down with wetness. I hear splashing from the shower, the deluge brings me down and I am underwater again.

You are right, I am late for work. I don't need to look at the clock on the bedside table. I know. But I still don't move, I can't. I hear you thud down the hallway, wet feet slapping against the tiles. You call to me, you say, 'Laura, get out of bed.' You're in the kitchen, slamming cupboard doors and slamming cups down on the worktop. Each loud sound makes my head pound, my head throb. I sink deeper into the pillow.

You come back into the bedroom. I hear you blow on the hot coffee and take your first sip. It sounds like water rushing through reeds. You splutter and dribble some on your beard. I can hear you slurp. 'You don't have time for a cup of coffee,' you say, 'so I didn't make you one.'

'I can't go to work today,' I say, into the pillow, my tongue licking and liking the taste of muddy water and algae seeping through the fabric.

You tell me I'm ridiculous and take another slurp of coffee and slam the cup down on the glass coaster on the bedside table. The coaster cracks, the coffee spills – 'Shit,' you whisper. I hate your guzzling breathy whispers and the coasters were a gift from your mother and I don't care if they smash.

I am pathetic, I am childish, I am ridiculous. I lift my head up from the pillow and look at you properly in the morning light, bright, your skin is luminous. I watch you wiping the spilled coffee with the corner of your towel. Love leaks from me. The shape of your back is beautiful. Your shoulders are broad, your arms are thick with muscles, veins stand like ropes wound round. In this light your skin is pale and speckled with freckles, tiny dark hairs curl at the nape of your neck, your long neck. I touch your neck, I weave my fingers into your hair. 'Stop,' you tell me in your lowest, coldest voice.

You get dressed and leave without saying anything more. I move around the memory of you in the room to gather my clothes and shoes. Your wet towel, puddles of coffee, worn socks, shorn hair. Things that belong to you. Your belongings, piled, strewn, blocking. This is how I live now. Navigating your stuff, careful not to knock things down, careful not to leave marks. Your hairs stick to my bare feet, there is dust in the corners of the room. This is how I live now, in this domestic disgust.

I rinse my dirty feet in the bathtub, in the dark. We do things in the dark since the light bulb blew and you won't change it and I can't change it. I can't reach. And there is nothing to see, we have both decided that. I brush my teeth. Whilst I brush, I pick up your toothbrush and feel the bristles between my thumb and forefinger. They are splayed out and soft, overused and old. Bristles like your whiskers. I rinse both brushes and drop them back in the glass. They cross one another.

I Am Blue

I tie my shoes outside under the street light. The light is orange and warm to settle the receding night and encourage the unsure day, white and weary, like me. I swing my bag on to my shoulder and step out from under the light. The air is mild, smells sweet for a moment. I close my eyes and think about being somewhere else. Like in my dream, in a forest with a lake in the clearing, the wind light and warm and blowing and sending me gifts of petals and green leaves, my hair shifting gently, drawing in breaths of blossom and grass. I feel tranquil and light like the air.

And then a car screeches past, a siren followed by an ambulance, motorbikes, more cars, smoke grease grit and growls erupting in the street. I open my eyes and start to walk into the growing day, the sky going from white to grey, bleeding pink from the rays of sunlight reaching up to make room in the sky for the sun to sit on a shelf of cloud. I try to love this part of the day because I won't see daylight for the next twelve hours. I try to love London but London doesn't love me, doesn't love itself. I love this morning light but I can't love the grime, the concrete, the dead pigeon. Pigeon, poor wings, what wings, detached, feathers clumped and matted, parting to let white bones protrude. Sickly white and shiny, they have been licked clean. The beak lies further along the street. Strangely, no blood on the concrete but sad feathers, scattered, stuck in litter. I look down for too long, looking for the other missing parts of the pigeon. I feel sad. Where are his gnarled feet? Poor Pigeon does get a little bit of my love, but I must keep some in reserve.

I walk down the steps into the station. The darkness inside is split with yellow strip lights. The man in the big coat and hat stands by the ticket machine. He is rubbing his hands together and shifting his weight from foot to foot, stamping on the dirty tiles. Over time, his stamping has caused cracks in the tiles and when he retires from his post or dies, there will be two big boot prints, two inches deep from where he has stood and stamped for so many years.

He smiles and nods when he sees me. I smile and nod back. He is the ticket-hall attendant but I have never seen him attend to anything other than trying to keep himself warm. I have never heard him speak, I have never seen him move, other than to rub his hands and stamp and shuffle. Even in the summer, he stands in his big coat, rubbing his hands together whilst people walk down into the darkness of the station hoping for relief from the singeing summer sun and sighing miserably when they hit a new wave, a new wall of stinking hot air from the trains and the tunnels below. He hasn't ever felt warm. His nose is long and blue.

I pass through the gate and step on to the escalator, I let it carry me down. The motion is smooth, a wind whips above me, the top of my head is blown, my fringe flies. I resist the urge to throw my arms out like wings. I think of Pigeon. If I fell from this height my bones would break, my wings would crumple. I watch the ground swallow the steps, one by one, as I glide closer. It would swallow me but I step off just in time and turn to the dismal platform. I walk to the place where I wait every day, opposite the flaking poster advertising breakfast cereal.

I am far away from everyone down here. I am far away from you. There is one other person down here, a figure at the end of the platform who waits. A face, white and drawn, eyes in shadow, indistinguishable. Dark clothes blending into the blackness of the tunnel. From this far away, just a face, but a tired folding body, just like mine.

I used to be afraid to take the train. So small, cramped, dirty, suffocating. I used to breathe in every time the train sped through a tunnel. Would we make it through the tiny opening, would the metal scrape the concrete, cut off the roof, cut off our heads? But the trains fit perfectly like banana skins or cotton socks. And now the vastness of the tunnels scares me. Huge, gaping black holes, rumbling pit-belly sounds that shake the ground, shake the lights hanging from chains. Tunnels connecting nothing but miles and miles of darkness. The figure at the edge is a speck and the tunnel is an open mouth, screaming or swallowing.

Grumbling sounds. Could be my empty stomach but then the screech of metal on metal signals a train speeding on the tracks. I take a step forward and watch the peeling corners of the poster flutter. The track is lit by the headlights of the train, I watch a little brown mouse clamber and clatter over the dirt-crusted metal and take cover as the train rattles closer. The train thrashes past me, I turn my head to see the figure with the white face, the white face, the white face with black eyes wide, and I watch as they step off the edge.

I Didn't Hear You

I leave my scream behind, the echo of it chases me as I run past open carriage doors. Passengers sleep, don't see me running, don't hear my panic. I reach the front of the train as the driver signals departure. I bang my bunched fists against the metal carriage. The driver peers at me through the dirty glass with narrow eyes, a puzzled frown.

'STOP!'

My voice is hoarse, thick with morning, dulled by the hum of the rumbling engine. The driver holds his hands up to me. He looks confused and scared, is he surrendering? Why is he moving so slowly? Why isn't he rushing to help or call someone? I unclench my fists. My hands are filthy and cold. Cold is creeping up on me. The driver opens the door, inching with caution.

'What's going on? I need to move the train. What are you doing?' His voice is deep and quiet with fear. Why is he afraid of me?

I am shaking, sweating, shivering, dishevelled.

'There was someone on the edge. They must have fallen on the track. Please help.' Doubt creeps up on me, a pinching finger of shame on my shoulder.

'Didn't you see?' He must have seen.

My forehead is pouring water but my mouth is dry and the words stick. He's not afraid now. He looks cross, his brow crinkles.

'What? What are you talking about? Why have you stopped my train?' His voice is now loud and sure.

'I saw someone. Standing on the edge. They went over.' They fell over. They jumped over.

His eyes widen, his stare follows the streams of sweat that wash horror over my face.

'You should take the next train, or go home. Do not get on my train.'

He closes the door, the metal slams and clacks as he locks it, his eyes still on me, still staring spotlights through the filthy window. The signal sounds and all the carriage doors close.

I Am Extremely Late Now

When the train pulls away, I grit my teeth, my body tenses, I wait to hear the squelch and crunch of a body breaking. But the sound of the engine is loud and I hear nothing but metallic shrieking. When the train is gone, I walk close to the edge of the platform, stoop low and peer over to see bloodied chunks of remains, but there is nothing but grit and tracks in blackness. Could the body have been thrown? Are they in there?

A cracking sound from overhead snaps me back out of the tunnel and I am surprised to find myself balancing unsteadily, rocking, a wisp of wind could blow me over the edge. A voice emerges from the cracking, crackling with panic, 'Passengers are reminded to remain behind the yellow line at all times,' a cough, a croak, 'Please step away from the platform edge. The next train will arrive in one minute.' I rise, carefully, disoriented, confused, and step backwards and keep walking until my back is against the wall. I saw them. I saw their face. But no one else saw. No evidence.

No remains. There must be a camera, video footage, something. But the driver saw nothing – no, the driver saw trouble. Troubled me.

The train pulls in, more passengers line the carriages. There are people on the platform, lots of people now that I didn't see or hear arrive. We wait for the carriage doors to open and step inside. I find a seat far away from others. I put my backpack on my lap and rest my head. The white face rolls around when I close my eyes. Did I imagine the whole thing? Yes, possibly, probably, I am tired, already on my last legs, and the day hasn't even started yet.

No time to think. I step off the train into a sea of people, I think of you as we surge towards the exit and sweep through the gate. I think of you rushing away as quickly as you can from me.

For the Next Twelve Hours, I Am Here

'I'm sorry I'm late,' I say, as I push through the swing doors, zipping up my crumpled uniform. She doesn't turn around, her shoulders slacken slightly, her head tilts, she looks at me sideways, her smile is small, her voice is quiet, 'It's okay, I'll let you off the hook, just this once.' She lifts her eyes and watches me tie my hair up into a knot on top of my head. She finishes writing the allocation on a sheet of paper, puts her pen in her pocket and hands the paper to me, turning to look fully at my flushed face. She puts a hand on my shoulder, straightens out my collar. 'You look tired,' she says, searching my face with her shiny kind eyes. 'You mean, I look like crap?' I ask. She just smiles. She taps the paper with her finger. 'I've given you the same as yesterday, is that going to be okay?' She brings her face close to mine. 'I'm so glad you came in, Sylvie called in sick overnight, again, but Rudy is here and the student is here and she's not bad.' She gives me a little poke, her eyes shimmer. 'She's working with Rudy, he'll keep her busy,' she says in a whispering chuckle. 'We'll be fine,' I say but I can't manage a smile. I need water, I need coffee. I wish I didn't have to be here.

I reach into my pockets and realise I'm wearing yesterday's uniform. I try to discreetly sniff the collar, raise my shoulder and twist my neck to smell under my arm. Not sweaty. But not fresh. I feel grim. I hate starting the day this way. I dig into the pockets for surprises. My name badge, a pen (bonus), a crumpled hand towel with a phone number scrawled on it (X-ray), a handful of saline ampoules (shit, thank goodness I didn't take home actual medication) and a single piece of chewing gum with a little coat of dust. I wipe the dust off and pop the gum in my mouth and let my teeth sink in. Glorious saliva pours, the tingle of strong mint floods my tongue. A small spurt of joy.

I see a silhouette in the frosted glass of the drug preparation room door. Dark blue and stretched, headless. I open the door on Rudy's tall form, head on his shoulders where it should be, almost touching the ceiling. He is hunched and crammed into the tiny room, squinting at his allocation sheet through thick specs, paper pressed to his palm, scribbling times and drawing lines.

'You're here. I'm glad,' he says. 'Jennifer is a fucking lunatic.'

I hand him the ampoules. 'Jennifer is okay,' I say, 'she's nice to me.'

'She's nice to you because you don't complain and you always look so …'

'So?'

'So, so – I don't know, with your big fucking eyes. I don't know, you always look innocent.'

'Earnest?'

'Too fucking good.'

Don't swear, I don't say to him.

'Can we do our pain meds together later?' I say. He takes his glasses off and puts his thumb and finger into the deep red ridges above his nose. He shuts his eyes and yawns. His mouth is huge and the smell of coffee and toothpaste drift out in a mist of moist breath. He nods with the yawn and reluctantly closes his mouth. The yawn looks like it feels good, warm and easy. I want to fold into it with him.

'Yes, but it's a long time until then.' He puts his hands on my shoulders and spins me around, navigating me through the doorway, around a drip stand and to the nurses' station. 'Here she is,' he says to Harriet.

Her eyes are bloodshot and wet, her lips are flaking. She grabs my wrist with rock-skinned hands, her knuckles are raw, sore, red tracking up her wrists, dotted with drying crusts of blood.

'Harriet, your hands!'

'It's okay, I'm off for the next five days, I just need to rest.' She pulls me down on to a chair beside her.

'We've had a bad night,' she lowers her voice and lowers her head towards the desk. She points a thin, splitting-skinned finger to the notes.

'Our baby is back in oxygen, but the cannula is rubbing the skin under his nose, it's so sore, I've kept him uncovered, he has cried all night. The doctor upped his morphine, fentanyl is going in, he desperately needs a pain review today. They want to do a scan but he's probably not safe for transfer. They should take him down to intensive care but intensive care won't take him because he's managing his airway, just. Mum has been awake with me most of the night. She wanted to change him but I did it, I told her to rest. She's shattered. He's shattered, he's settled now but keep an eye on him, Laura, the consultant wants you in the meeting today to make a plan. It's not looking good for our little mate. He needs weighing twice today, he's puffed up like a little piece of popcorn. Oh, and the dressing on his central line is peeling and needs changing. He's got morphine and some fat bolus doses, I've pushed that button all night long. Have you had a coffee? You look as rough as I feel. Have you got little Bud next door too? He's been easy overnight, slept and dreamt. He's cute. Dad snores and smells a bit. But he shouldn't give you much trouble. They want him to try an oral feed. I'm not sure if Dad will help much. He didn't get up once in the night to try and feed, just left me to tube it.

'Oh, that's a shame. Where is his mama?' I ask.

'She was with him when he was admitted but she got completely freaked out in the cubicle. She said it was spooky and claustrophobic so she's at home with the other children,' she says, nodding. 'But she is right, it is spooky and claustrophobic, I couldn't stay in there. Okay, have fun! See you next week!'

She slides her chair back and stands. She gives my shoulder a little squeeze on her way out. 'Thanks, Harriet,' I say, sinking in my chair. Sinking in. Everything else is sucked up and stored, in space, somewhere, suspended outside of this endless day. Tiredness falls off like shrivelled snakeskin, it will hang over the doorway and wait for me until the end of the day. Hang and wait to engulf my withered body, wrap me up and crush.

I draw out my day in twelve long lines. It helps to know where the end is. Jennifer turns the lights up and the room glows, synthetic sunshine. The student stretches her arms out, I see her peering over the top of the raised desk, she is looking at the lines I chase out with drugs and dressings and doctors. 'That looks complicated,' she says. I look up at her. She looks fresh and young and hopeful.

'Can I help you today, Laura?'

Yes.

'I only have bed 6.'

'You mean you only have *Florence* today.'

Blush rushes through her cheeks.

'I only have Florence today,' she whispers. 'I could help you.'

'Yes, I have to bath and weigh my baby first thing. If you get your safety checks done and you've written up your meds for Rudy, then I could really do with an extra pair of hands. Thank you.'

She nods, her perky ponytail whips. I manage a tiny smile of encouragement and she smiles back, beaming, she bounces away.

Poor baby, poor baby, what will happen today? I fold the paper and put it in my pocket. No time, so time to start. I stand at the window, put my face close to glass and cup my hands around my eyes to block out the light. The baby is a small mound in the cot. His skin is silvery in the shadowy room. Ghastly tentacles of gleaming plastic flow out of his nose and his chest, leads leading to lines on the monitor, furious, frenzied blue lines tracing signs of life, the sign of a heart trying hard, running across the black face of the monitor and dropping off the screen into oblivion. Mother is a big mound in deeper shadows sleeping on the bed by the window. She is bound in blankets, glowing green from the light of the television.

I turn away from the window. Jennifer is looking through notes at the desk. 'Harriet thinks they'll make an end-of-life plan for Danny,' I say, tilting my head towards the window. She nods. She looks up at me, her face full of sadness. 'Do you think he'll last long enough to make it home?' she asks. It's hard to tell. She stands next to me. I point to the monitor. 'Look how tired he is.' We both stare at ourselves sharply reflected in the glass. I can see the black circles around my eyes, swirling pools, muddy ponds. I'd better make a start. I leave Jennifer looking and quietly open the door to the cubicle.

This Will Never Be Too Much for Me

The antechamber is lit only by the red flashing sensor in the ceiling and the light from the corridor dropping through two inches of glass running the length of the door. The red light blinks, signalling the filtering of the air I brought in with me. The red light signals the beginning of my ritual. I peel back the corner of an apron and pull it from the roll. The flashing red looks like blood splattering across the shiny white plastic. I tear it from the perforated line and put it over my head, tying it tightly around my waist. The plastic scores the skin on my neck which will be sore later. I run my hands under scorching water. It cools after a few seconds and I squeeze the soap dispenser. Fifteen seconds of scrubbing, wrist to tips, thinking of the filth on the train carriage door I touched this morning. A speck could infect Danny. I wash my hands again and dry them with rough paper towels that tear across my skin. When they are dry I put on the blue vinyl gloves that fit tightly. I feel my hands begin to sweat and re-wet themselves.

When the red light stops blinking, I open the door silently, squeeze through a tiny gap and close the door, guiding the handle until it clicks quietly. I tiptoe to the cot, my apron swishes but the sound is lost in the hissing, whistling flow of oxygen. There is a low dip-dip-beep, dip-dip-beep from the monitor, dip-dip-beep, dip-dip-beep. Danny has wriggled his fat little foot and loosened the grasp of the sensor probe on his toe. I silence the alarm and lower the side of the cot, the metal shrieks and I pause and hold my breath and hope it hasn't woken Danny's mum. I listen for her quiet sleep breathing and slowly let the side all the way down, controlling the shriek to a mouse's squeak.

This moment, this silent morning when mums and dads are sleeping, I am here, I am working in the dark. I slip in, I ease myself between them and the crushing weight of their worry. I spread my palms, my dry skin cracks, but I gladly take the weight and I brace myself. I spread my arms, my tired arms tremble. But it's never too much, I can take more.

These early hours are precious. Peace is present, but wrinkled like the foreheads of the drifting dreamers. Drifting, unsteadily shifting from exhaustion to the recognition and relief of rest. I wish it could be longer. I wish I could smooth out the wrinkles, let the peace be permanent and true.

This moment, this small moment, is for a mother whose son won't heal. She wants to be awake for it all, she wants to spend time while she has it, with him, but really there is no time. I try not to think about the conversation we need to have when she wakes.

I position myself at the head of the cot, Danny's face is puffy and white, his tiny nose is turned upwards, with the pressure of the nasal cannula and the feeding tube filling his nostrils. His lips are dusky pink, his mouth puckered and open.

His pale eyelashes lie flat like trampled cornfields against a blue sky of blistered eyelids. I unbutton his too-big Babygro. Sadness slows my motions as I realise the suit won't ever fit him, he won't ever fully grow into it. The skin beneath the soft cotton is almost translucent, thinly stretched over his curved ribcage and bulbous belly. I place my hand lightly on his stomach and count the breaths he takes. The heat of his little body barely meets mine through the thickness of my glove. His chest is slow to rise, his two little lungs are rubber balloons never blown.

I place two fingers in the crook of his elbow and press to feel his pulse. His skin here is too dense and oedematous, I can't feel anything so I trace my fingers along the bone to his wrist. His pulse is bold and bounces too fast. I count for a minute. I work my eyes down his tiny body. His toes are cold and the colour of dust. I rub each one between my thumb and forefinger to warm them. They are so tiny. When blood begins to flow back into them, I reattach the probe and watch the numbers on the monitor rise and sink and settle. I put a blanket over his feet to keep them warm.

I pull my pen-torch out of my top pocket and point the light over the peeling dressing. I bend closer to see the white coiled tube, white shining plastic lost against his porcelain skin. I follow the coil with my eyes, turning turning in, a line into a tiny red ring of skin, and if I follow it further the redness of internal flesh, the pink and squelching red, darker, more muscular, into a big vein and there it sits. Blood out, drugs in.

I lift his body gently, my gloves slip against the moisture on his skin, tricky to grip. He is soaking wet, his Babygro feels damp. I bring a gloved hand to my nose to smell, to check he has not wet through his nappy, although I know Harriet would have changed him during the night. The smell of peaty outdoor dampness wafts towards me. Last night's dream floats upwards, tries to resurface; I press it down, push it back under. I inhale again, and smell mud mixed with chemicals. Toxicity drips out of him and I'll pour more into him. I wonder if the doctors will reduce some of his medication. He doesn't smell one tiny bit like a baby.

I tilt his body again to look at his back. There are two pink rectangular indentations where the ends of the line have sat snug and comfortably in his bloating flesh. Morphine slides down the line, feeding him a low slow trickle. There is an 'S' shape on his skin where the line has snaked up his back and nestled, nested. I rub the redness gently and shake my head. He is marked now and will be for a while. Poor baby. Okay. I settle him back and button up his Babygro, threading the line through a buttonhole. I feel its thinness with my fingers and feel it all the way to the pump. My fingers are stopped by a Perspex shield. Big plastic monstrous machinery, grey and whirring, all locks and corners, lines and blinking lights. The big green button hangs down from the metal stand on a thick black lead. The light is not lit and the morphine is locked out, I watch the timer tick on the grimy display screen. I note down on my folded paper how much is left in the syringe and when it will need changing. I wipe down the screen with a wet wipe, scrub away ancient crusted drips and sticky spills.

As I begin to slide the cot side back into place, his eyes scrunch up, lines crease his swollen eyelids, his breath rasps and creaks as he cries. I have unsettled him. His chest rattles with loose mucus. 'Shh,' I say, placing one hand on his stomach and reaching for the suction tube on the wall behind the cot. I flip the switch and tug the tube, freeing the suction catheter from the plastic wrapping. I look at the canister and see floating green foam that has collected through the night. I changed the canister yesterday, his secretions are increasing. I place the catheter gently in his open mouth and clear the collections of spittle and mucus. The whooshing sound of the vacuum sucks up his cracking cry. I flip the switch again and the sound stops. His cry subsides, his breaths return to soft chugs. The oxygen saturations on the monitor rise slightly. I tap his tummy and shush hush him back to sleep.

If You Will Make All That Noise

The door rattles in the frame, the clattering shakes me, breaks me out of the soothing moment that I was swaying in, soothing Danny to sleep. I stop tapping his tummy and hold my breath. I listen to the student shuffling in the antechamber, the slopping of the water in the sink, the splashes against the plastic apron she has ruffled in a hurry to pull over her head. I quickly but quietly shift the cot side up and secure the catches. I tiptoe to the door, I glance at Danny's mum, she hasn't stirred, despite the racket carrying through the room. The bin lid slams and the door handle turns. As the student bursts through, I step towards her and press my finger tightly to my lip, showing her a silent exaggerated SHHH. She jumps back, her eyes are wide, terrified. She slowly brings her finger to her own mouth and nods.

I drop my hand and beckon her towards the cot. She stands across from me and I demonstrate how to pull the cot side down without making any noise. She mimics my actions and nods, her ponytail swishing over the plastic apron around her neck. She smiles at me. Her white young teeth are eerie in the luminous blue light of the monitor. I smile back, looking at her face fully for the first time. Her face is heart-shaped and eager. Her skin is pale and flecked with freckles in all the right places, perfectly settled by skin-kissing sunrays. Her eyes are brown or blue or green but her pupils are so dilated with joy and wonder they are round black shining balls. She is taking me in. She is taking him in. She stands straight, her uniform is white and ironed. She doesn't know what to do with her hands. She could be me, standing there. That used to be me. My ponytail used to swish. But her face is so full of eagerness. I never had that. She was born, she came out of her mother singing. Everything heart-shaped. This is all she ever wanted. And now she's here, no more longing. She can't bounce. Her heart is too big and will get in the way. She will learn to float. I wish she could keep her eagerness. I will her to keep it.

I feel bad that I can't remember her name. I feel annoyed that she isn't wearing her name badge. I watch her lowering her head to look closer at Danny. She is gentle. She lightly touches a gloved finger to Danny's tiny clenched fist. She looks up at me, her face full of alarm. 'He feels cold,' she whispers, 'and spongy. He is like a little sponge.'

I nod my head slowly. She looks at me, into my eyes, and she knows. Our eyes open and close together, our eyes fill full of tears we won't cry yet but the wetness is there and we glisten together. We wait in the quiet. She waits for me. But it is quiet and I want to stay like this and show her calmness so that she can be calming.

Crack crack crack the window cracks, the sound is sharp and we both turn our heads towards it. Jennifer is there, her hand raised to the glass, confusion covering her face. 'What's wrong? What's happened?' she calls through the intercom. I shrug my shoulders. 'What's going on? What do you mean?' I say, my voice hushed; I glance behind me, Danny's mum doesn't stir. The student looks scared. 'You pulled the crash bell, don't you hear it?'

I step towards the window and look above Jennifer's head. The alarm bell is lit, the red light reflects in the glass across the corridor. I look at the wall behind Danny's cot.

It's impossible.

The alarm is protruding from the wall, triggered and glowing. I squeeze myself behind the space and push the button back into the wall. It is stiff, it is rarely used. It is impossible. Impossible to move without forceful fingers. 'Jen, it's okay,' I say through the intercom. 'I don't know how that happened. We're fine in here, Danny is sleeping.' The confusion on her face gives way to concern. 'That's so strange. I thought something had happened, the alarm made me jump.' 'I'm sorry,' I say. 'I really don't know. We're just standing here.' She nods. 'We're coming out now,' I say. 'We're going to get things ready to change his dressing.'

I'll See You in a Minute

We leave the room in silence, remove our aprons and wash in silence. Outside the room, the student pours. 'It wasn't me, I swear,' she says. She looks scared. 'It's okay,' I say. I touch her shoulder. 'How could it have been you? You didn't pull the alarm. It must be a trip in the wires, or something.' She looks up at the little light bulb above the door. 'I didn't even hear the alarm,' she says, 'did you?' I shake my head. Jennifer is back at the nurse's station. 'Jen, we didn't even hear the alarm,' I say. 'Well, it was certainly going off out here. Although Rudy didn't even come out to see what was going on, I'll have to speak to him,' she says. She seems annoyed. 'I can't explain it. I'll phone the estates department and see if they can take a look at it today,' I say. She sighs. 'No, it's all right, I'll do it. You have enough to do today,' she says, a little lighter.

'Wait here,' I say to the student. 'Unless Rudy needs you. I'm just going to check on my patient next door quickly.' She nods, her eyes are fixed on the window to Danny's room.

Again, the shredding and shedding of skin as I scrub my hands, the silent dance to the bedside. His breaths, his beats, settled and soothed. No trouble here. On his way to health. He has blood in his cheeks, the blood is beautiful because it circulates quickly around his body, rising to the surface of his skin in beautiful pink rounds. He has white-blond hair. He is not ready to be woken yet. Dad snores and Harriet is right, the smell of microwave meals and cigarettes has settled over his bed like a cloud. I wave the imaginary fumes away from the baby. I'll come back later.

You Need Me to be Clean

The student is waiting for me as I exit the antechamber. Her focus is restored, she's back to her original purpose of eating me up. 'Come on then, let's go to the treatment room and get what we need.' She is full to burst but still sucking, I feel her sucking at me, slurping up my energy, starving hungry. The hairs on my arms bristle, I am prickled by her attention and in a prickly voice ask her where her name badge is. I regret it instantly as she unravels in front of me. First she flings her hands up to her breast pockets, she pats down the front of her uniform, fingering her pockets in a frenzy. Her eyes are pierced with wounds and worries, her posture creases, I feel sorry. 'It's here, somewhere, it might be in my bag, oh no I've left it at home, oh, oh, oh.'

There was nothing to be gained and I crumple with her. 'It's just because you are new here, so that the parents can identify you. We ask everyone for identification when they come into the department, we should also set an example.' I try to make my voice warmer. I feel bad for putting a pin in her. I exhale all my hot horrible air and try and start again.

'So, what do you think we need for this dressing?'

She answers me cautiously, correctly.

Your Pain is Worse Than I Knew

Danny is still sleeping but his mother is awake, she is leaning over the cot cooing and stroking his cheek. 'Good morning, Tracy,' I say, 'I have a student working with me today, is it okay if she helps me with Danny's dressing?' I incline my head towards the student who has taken up her position as my shadow.

'Morning, yes I met Samantha the other day.'

Samantha. Thank goodness.

'Hello again,' says Samantha, beaming big bright rays around the room.

Samantha. I'll write it down.

Tracy's eyes are black and puffy. The dark circles of sleep deprivation warping her cheeks rival mine. Mine are ponds, hers are stormy seas. But light movements of her lips, the little smile at her son that sends ripples of dimples in her cheeks show hope. She is younger than me, she is a mother. My hand grasping the tray of sterile dressings begins to quiver, my breath aches to escape.

'Tracy, the doctors are going to have a meeting today, they want you to be there and they've asked me to be there too.' I speak gently, I try to disguise with softness the sound of the lump forming in my throat. She looks up at me, there is no fear or sadness in her eyes. She doesn't know that there is no solution. Or she does and she's being strong.

Tracy picks up her baby. I help her navigate the wires and tubes. We move a chair to the window and lower her into it, with pillows on her lap and a blanket to keep warm. She rests Danny on the pillows and holds him close to her chest. She rocks him gently and I push the button, I give him a dose to keep him comfortable. I pause to watch for a moment while she whispers to him, brushing his cheek with a finger, the leads and wires coiling around her arms, they are tethered.

We work together, we synchronise quickly. We strip the sheets from the mattresses, scrub them down with wet soapy cloths. They dry as we unfold fresh linen. The crisp whiteness of the sheets satisfies me. As we lift them taut into the air I hope to smell the fake flowery fragrance of fresh-washed sheets but all I smell is dry sterility, the faint smell of steel, steam and slight scorching. We smooth out the sheets over the mattress and fold the corners, our arms waving, our bodies bending, we are like synchronised swimmers and I can't help but smile. Samantha grins back at me, she is relaxed and happy to be helping. I walk around to her side of the cot to check the folds of the sheet in the corners. 'Did Rudy teach you how to do these?' She blushes and nods. They're pretty good, I'm impressed. I roll a soft flannel blanket sprinkled with a pattern of coloured stars and arrange it like a little doughnut for Danny to snuggle into.

Tracy begins to undress Danny in her lap. She knows the routine. 'I'll change his line dressing whilst he's on your lap, he's settled there and I can reach just fine.' She looks pleased. 'He is comfy, isn't he?' She gives a little laugh. 'Snug-as-a-bug-in-a-rug.' I remove my gloves and wash my hands thoroughly. They are already abnormally red as I wring the water off them and reach for a paper towel. I wince as I apply alcohol gel and sterile gloves. Samantha removes the old dressing, it lifts with no resistance. I clean with chemicals, swirling in circles over the pink exit skin. I carefully lift the line, scrubbing over and under, over and under, over his chest and under his arm. When his skin has dried I coil the line, stick it quickly down with strips and then peel back the sheet of film. The trickiest bit. We all hold our breath whilst I position the flimsy film over the coil and one two three press it down, pinching in the middle and stretching out the edges. I smooth it out with my fingertips, making sure the film has stuck fast. 'Perfect,' says Tracy and she pecks Danny's nose with puckered lips. He doesn't stir. I get up from the floor, the blood flows back into my toes, my knees and legs ache from being crouched for too long. Samantha sees me huff and puff, I smile and say my knees aren't what they used to be.

I Need More Than Your Hand on My Shoulder

Rudy scares the shit out of me with his face pressed up against the glass, warped and weird, one eye staring, his breath fogging from a grotesque grin. I slam into the door and drop my tray on the floor. 'You scared the shit out of me!' I say, putting my palm over the window to cover his face. The student rushes to the door behind me, looking at me through glass. 'Are you okay?' she mouths; I nod and motion to her to go back to Tracy and help bath the baby. I look back to Rudy and he is holding his belly, laughing and rolling in the corridor. I wash my hands quickly and pick up the tray, throw open the door and fold my arms, staring at him. I tap his arm with my tray and push past to the treatment room.

'Don't be like that, it was just a joke, I was trying to spook you.'

It worked.

'Will you check this for me, please?' He slides a tray in front of me, full of glass vials, water, needles and lines.

I sigh, loudly. 'I'm not sticking my hand in that tray.'

He rolls his eyes and picks out two broken glass vials and two syringes. He slips the drug chart in front of my face and points. 'Antibiotics due now,' he flips the chart, 'and she's had all of her anti-emetics, but she's white as a sheet, says she feels sick and I am not cleaning up any chunks today.' He screws up his face, I can't help but laugh. 'Sign, please.' He hands me a pen. 'How is little Florence?' I ask, I haven't seen her for a long time. He shrugs. 'She looks good to me, but Mum is still fussing.'

'I've got your student. Samantha? She's helping Tracy with bathtime.'

'She'll be ecstatic!' He bounces around the tiny room, knocks into a shelf of fluid bags. They drop, one by one, to the floor, the weight of sandbags, the crashing wet sound of the sea. 'Oops, I'll come back for those.' He beckons me out of the room and down the corridor to Florence's room. I stand in the window with the drug chart as he washes his hands.

The curtains are drawn and the room is bright. Florence and her mother are sat in the bed wearing matching pink robes. Florence is tucked in her mother's arms. They are both watching the television.

Rudy enters the room and flicks the switch for the intercom, he gives me a thumbs-up. Mum straightens up, pats her hair down and beams at him. He points to me in the window and I give a little wave. She smiles and waves, leans and whispers in Florence's ear. Florence's eyes are wide, absorbing the bright colours of the cartoon. She blinks, turns for a second with a small smile for me, and turns back to the television, eyes wide, mouth wider. Mum looks at me apologetically. I say gently through the intercom, 'Florence, you look very pretty today.' Mum mouths 'Thank you', not knowing that I can hear the music from the cartoon and Rudy's chatter. She puts her lips together and kisses Florence's little bald head. I can see her eyes watering but I smile at her and she nods and shuts her eyes tight, she squeezes Florence tighter.

'Here we go, my sweet,' says Rudy. 'Can you tell me your date of birth, so Laura knows this medicine is meant for you and she can sign your chart.' She keeps her eyes glued to the screen but says her full name, date of birth, hospital number, she unties her dressing gown, puts her hand under her nightshirt and pulls out the long lumens of her central line and holds them, ready to be plugged in. He chuckles. I sign the chart and wave goodbye.

As I walk away, the thought of Florence before comes close, falls like curtains over my eyes, falls like the strands of her beautiful shining auburn hair, long and flowing. Falling. Falling. Falling out. Mum cried immediately. The loss was thick.

Strands tangled in the hairbrush. She wept loudly out into the corridor and I ran to her because I thought Florence had died. She threw the hairbrush at me. Not hard, not to harm me. It skidded across the floor, it looked like a creature, like a crush of road-kill, warm, red and wasted. I brought it back to her and held her whilst she sobbed. Not yet. Please, not yet.

More hair through the night, from tossing and turning, clumps wound round the bed rails, tufts on the pillow, red and golden nests. Florence was curious, examined them, tangled them round her little fingers. But she did not cry. She did not say a word.

I came with clippers before bathtime. Mum wept again and scooped the hair as it fell into a pillow case. I whispered to Florence in her ear over the hum of the razor. I told her she was strong like a tree and her red hair was autumn leaves falling.

Mum slept with the pillowcase held to her chest. I was there in the morning when Florence woke up, she raised her hands to her head and felt with all her fingers running over the soft skin. Her little mouth fell open and she reached for me. She held my hand and said, 'Am I an egg now?'

Sit with Me

There is bliss in the silence of the staffroom. And the sun shining through the window, the hot light falling on my face, the heat from the seat and if I could close my eyes and if I could sleep for a minute. I don't dare and I drink my coffee. I keep the cup to my lips. The bitter wisps waft up my nose, stings because it is so strong and so hot. It keeps me awake. I sit staring across the room, out into the hallway, waiting for Jennifer or Rudy or Samantha to come and break my break any minute now.

Two string beans stride down the corridor but back-step when they see me and stop in the doorway. Both tall, both thin, one the image of the other twenty years before, or twenty years later. Grey hair still thick, spectacles slipping down a gently wrinkled nose, years of tired in the creases around his eyes, years of tired in the creases around his mouth, eyes of endless kindness. He looks through his specs at me and says: 'Laura, good morning, you're here again.'

47

The second face is thinner, the hair thicker. I see the lines around the eyes and mouth, but they are less furrowed, the mouth has less to be sorry for. The specs are straighter. He says nothing but he smiles and turns pink.

'Good morning, Dr Lucas, Dr Wilfred,' I say, watching Wilf's pink turn red and roll down his cheeks. 'Dr Lucas, I'm looking after Danny today.'

'Yes, good, and you know we will be speaking to his mother, it's not good, poor little chap, we think it is close to the end and we won't be doing more.' He folds in the middle, he is now half his height, weighed down. He feels the hopelessness heavily. We are all paper aeroplanes today, folding and unfolding, refolding to be sharper, to fly and succeed, but our aim is slightly off, one wing slightly bigger than the other, thrust into the air, tearing through the air, to wobble and nosedive and ripped up in the end because we didn't make it. This is how we feel.

'Do you want me to be at the meeting? To support Tracy? Danny's father won't be coming.'

'Yes please, you are essential for this discussion.' He takes his specs off, folds them into his top pocket and squeezes the bridge of his nose between his long fingers. He shuts his eyes. Wilf is watching him.

'Do you want a cup of tea? I'll bring it to the office,' I say. He doesn't open his eyes but he nods and says yes please.

Shoulders stooped, he shuffles backwards and turns and walks away. To straighten himself up, to shake off the sadness. Wilf walks towards me, to speak, to say something, but he stops and stands at the counter. I stand next to him and take two mugs from the cupboard. He says nothing, just stands near. I can feel his heat. His shirtsleeves are rolled up. He smells like cotton and soap and sweat. He smells like hard work. He watches me, he is a watcher. He says, 'You make nice tea,' and he leaves.

If I Wasn't Prepared, You Didn't Stand a Chance

Walking in, I know it's wrong. All wrong. The light is too bright, the air is too hot. The chairs are set out in a circle but the circle is too small and the room is too big. And this big room is brimming with death and it's too late to do anything because I'm dazzled by the sun shining through the window, so strong, and the strangeness of the furniture and Tracy has followed me into the room and sat down in the circle.

The board on the wall pinned with pictures of patients, piles and piles of smiles, is leering and sneering. Mocking smiles of the children who left, who healed and went home, and worse, the smiles of those who stayed, could not leave, have not left, have died. Shining sunny siren smiles. Tracy sees me staring at the pictures, she looks and smiles and asks me if all those children are well and went home and I lie and say yes. I lie looking into the last smiling face of a lost little one. Tracy smiles and I am stabbed through with guilt. Knife stuck in to the hilt. My mouth is dry, my words are whispers when I turn and see the tea set laid out on the little tray and ask her if she would like a cup. Yes please, milk and two sugars. Someone has put milk in the milk jug. Someone has arranged the teacups on saucers with handles all pointing in the same direction. There are fucking biscuits. The china is bone white with blood-red flowers running over the rims, dripping down the sides. This is the death china. This is brought out for families when their children die. This is supposed to show respect. This strange, ancient crockery has only ever touched the lips of those who are touched with death. And Danny is not dead yet. The flesh on my shaking hands crawls and controls the movements I make to pour tea and spill milk and stir sugar.

This is where I get a grip. This is when I strain for strength. Dr Lucas and Wilf walk in, split off and sit either side of Tracy. I am relieved to see Dr Lucas sitting straight up tall in his chair. He has uncreased his face, he has combed his hair, his mouth is serious but soft. Wilf has unrolled his sleeves and buttoned the cuffs. Dr Lucas looks at me and nods. I pour them tea too, I don't take a cup, thinking forward to the free hands needed for the full collapse.

Scraping chairs and clinking china. Dr Lucas clears his throat and begins.

It Was Better Than I Thought/It Was Worse Than I Thought

My shoulder is soaked through. I hold her tightly. Her body jerks and jolts as the wails come in waves. Beginning low, growling, guttural, surging upwards, skeleton shaking, escaping as she flings her head, flips her neck back, hope it doesn't snap, her mouth is wide open, wet. I hold her so that she doesn't fall to the floor. She's not ready to be soothed yet, so my arms remain rigid, we don't rock.

Her sucking swallowing shrieking is childlike and terrifying. I am worried she will choke. I loosen my grasp slightly, she gasps, sucks in air, swallows snot and tears, coughs, and I know what is coming next. She coughs and coughs and spews out the grief. And mucus. And tea. Watery and running. The tea is still hot. I feel it soak through my tunic. The smell is acrid, acidic, a smell of sugar and sour milk and nicotine. I breathe through my mouth.

Tracy is trembling still but the sick has shocked her and the shrieking stops. She pulls away from me slowly. Her hair clings to her sweat-soaked face.

'I'm so sorry,' she says in a croaking whisper. She swallows hard and winces. I feel the burning with her in my own throat. She keeps her eyes low like a told-off child. I reach my hand out and touch her arm.

'It's okay,' I say softly. 'Don't you worry about this. Why don't you go and splash some water on your face and then go and get some air?'

She nods, still avoiding my eyes, but now watching the steady drips of sick from the hem of my tunic to the floor. I am aware of the puddle of brown spreading around my shoes.

When she closes the door behind her, I close my eyes, I can't help the folding of my face, I feel the tears, they are there, they are ready, I try to bite them back. I hold my breath, I am about to break. I am about to fling myself into a sorry sob but I hear voices in the corridor, so I pull it back with a sharp breath. Rudy and Jennifer are there suddenly in the doorway. Their expressions clash. Rudy's tall straight form shatters, his laughter splinters me with broken glass. Jennifer, full of pity, rushes at me with paper towels, she takes my hand and helps me step over the pool of sick. She starts to dab at my tunic but has to pinch her nose and turn away.

'I can't, I'm sorry, Laura, I can't do adult puke,' she says, still pinching. She has turned green.

Rudy is wiping away the fat tears that have formed. His laugh still echoes around the room.

'Rudy, go and be helpful, will you? Go and look after Laura's babies whilst she goes and cleans herself up,' says Jennifer.

He leaves the room chuckling, 'I don't do adult puke either.'

I am slick with sick. I am stained with grief. I'll wash but it won't wear away. Grief will be worn like a cloak, will drag along behind me, heavy.

I take a linen sack to the changing room with me. Stripping off my sopping uniform, I realise the sick has soaked through to my bra. I take it off and hang it on a peg. I stand in my knickers and soap my shoulders and as much of my back as I can reach.

I rinse the suds off under the cold shower, too impatient to wait for the water to heat. With a rough white towel I furiously rub my skin dry. It scratches and feels good. I put on my jeans and top and head down to the basement, to the laundry room in search of scrubs or a spare uniform.

I Take a Quiet Minute

There is a magnetism to the little chapel that draws me to it. No, it doesn't draw me, I am propelled. I am pushed towards the closed oak doors, my arm is led to the brass handle, I reach for it with outstretched fingers but the stretch is not my own. The oak is ancient and chipped, it has absorbed years of prayers and light and life. It is yellow and it gleams. My hand on the brass handle feels the cold of hundreds of old hands. I lean with weight to push the door open. When I draw my hand back from the handle my skin zings, the smell of metal is sharp and lingers.

I could be anywhere in the world.

My feet are quiet on the carpet, a strange change from the echoing steps on the tiled corridor floors or creaking or squeaking on the linoleum in the ward, just mopped, wet and shining, soles sticking until the floor is dry.

The deep green carpet is lush and thick like forest ferns. There are faint footprints in the fibres. I am glad that someone else has been here today. The doors have closed behind me. All hospital sounds are shut out. There are no sounds in. But this is not silence. This is a breath taken, this is a wave drawn back. The chapel is waiting for a song or waiting for a prayer. I am waiting too. How I long for sound.

I am outside in. The chapel stood here long before the hospital. It was always small and had a little cemetery beside it. They moved it when the hospital was built, scooped up whole and set down somewhere, brought back years later, piece by piece, bricks, and then the windows put in. I read that somewhere. And now a capsule, walls inside walls.

The windows are lit, light streaming in, in all colours, rays of coloured ribbon, but light from where, I don't know. I can make out the faint lines of bricks behind the windows. The colours are vivid, but the light is not shining down from heaven. It is artificial, but pretty all the same. I walk between the pews to look closer at the pictures depicted in the glass. Jesus is here, a peachy babe, hair perfectly golden with blue-sky eyes. Bright-white angels with pink cheeks. Shepherds in green and brown shawls, little lambs, and the Three Wise Kings, crowned in purple and red, their arms outstretched, heavy with gifts. The scene wraps around the room, wraps around me, makes me feel warm, makes me feel almost cheerful, the colours tingling my tired eyes.

The windowsills are lined with teddy bears, they are lined up, ready to join the procession of the Wise

Kings. Every surface of the chapel is covered with stuffed bears. Over-stuffed with stuffed bears and other creatures. They feel like friends to me. Their softness makes the room feel like a play pit. I could sink in here and sleep. I walk along the wall and reach out and pick up a bear in yellow dungarees. His fur is the colour of my hair, his eyes are black and shiny. As I pull him away from his friends, dust coats my arm and I cry out as a big black spider with thick legs drops on to the carpet. I drop the bear and the spider scuttles away, somewhere underneath it. The thickness of the legs, their silent emerging from behind the bear, makes my skin creep as if the spider crawls upon me. Its blackness is a trope, a trick of the light, my mind. In real life I know the spider is not black. It is more sinister than that. It is brown, a particular shade, grown over time to be camouflage against dark wood and shadows. It grows like a skin on undrunk coffee. It is the colour of the underside of a picture frame. It is the exact shade of the darkness between the bear and the carpet. Indistinguishable from shadow. I raise my foot, hovering it over the bear's face. I am ready to stamp the fucking daylights out of that spider. I am ready to see the vile oozing from its hideous fat body, see a leg or two detached and splayed. The bear stares up at me. There is sadness in those shining eyes. I think about the child who once loved that bear, squeezed it tight. I bring my foot back down to the floor and step back from the windowsill. I didn't see it before, but I see it now. I tilt my head so that the light catches the little creatures in a different way. They are now all illuminated. They have a sickly sheen from fine layers of silver dust and cobwebs. I step back and look at them. They are not friends any more. Hundreds of pairs of black shiny plastic eyes stare. Worse than that, some of them have buttons for eyes. They are empty. Their empty stares cast a spell of sadness over me, I have to sit down on a pew. I finger the cover of a colourful children's prayer book, my fingertip falling into the groove of the letter 'P'.

These bears all used to belong. They were loved, hugged, dropped and caught. They were tucked up in bed and sat down to tea. And their love was cut off and they were brought here, set on the shelves as tributes. Dust clings to them desperately like children used to. And with the children gone they sit here and wait, love and play stored up in them, the energy from them is palpable, they bristle, their eyes staring, they look at me longingly.

I flip open the prayer book and find a verse for friends. I whisper it with my head bent, the words fizz and dissipate in the air. I hope the prayer finds the bears or the lost children. I close my eyes and say words for Danny. I ask God to hold him tight, to take him and to love him, to draw the pain out of him. I ask Him to place the pain on me instead. I am shaking as I speak. The blackness behind my eyes is vast, I fall into it, trembling.

When I open my eyes I am startled because the blackness is still there. A silent swish of black material, swiftly shifting and then sailing on the sea of green carpet. I look up and see the black robes swaying. The chaplain is moving towards the altar. With another person present, the chapel seems bigger. The robes are strangely black and strangely formal for this tiny children's church. With their head bent towards the glowing Baby Jesus, it's hard to tell if the chaplain is a woman or a man. I think to speak but I don't want to disturb their prayers, so I sneak out of the pew and tiptoe across the carpet. As I walk I wonder where the cemetery is now. I step carefully as if over tiny graves. I glance back at the altar as I open the old oak doors but the chaplain is no longer praying. The chaplain is no longer there.

It Took Your Blood on My Blood to Believe

For the rest of the shift I'm wearing scrubs the colour of dried blood. Deep red and rusty. The waistband is tight and itches. My belly shows when I stretch my arms up to hang the fluid bags on the hooks that dangle down from the ceiling. I am disturbed by these hooks, how they look, too large, too shiny, how the chains clang together when I reach up to hang, my arms together, my belly showing, skin scored with pink scratches, my body marked with irritation, from head to toe in this old red starched cloth, I look like a dead animal, hanged to dry out. Jennifer stares through the glass at this slaughter-house scene. She enters as I finish hanging the last fluid bag.

'Do you need me?'

Yes.

'Dr Lucas has stopped the nutrition, but said I could put up some slow fluids,' I say, uncertainly.

'Yes, that's fine,' says Jennifer. 'I can check them for you and do you want to do his pain meds too now?'

'Yes, can we get them out of the way? I was going to wait for Rudy but he's been a real dick today.'

We stand side by side at the bench, reaching for syringes, unwrapping needles, little wrists flicking as we dissolve the drugs into salt-smelling solutions. Our movements are mirrored perfectly. Jennifer smiles at me and does a little twirl.

'Who says nursing isn't an art?'

Who does say that?

She holds the tray whilst I wash my hands. The skin on my knuckles isn't broken yet but it's red as red, as red as my scrubs. We are close together in the antechamber, I feel her breath at the nape of my neck. She watches me washing and I feel self-conscious, like she might scold me at any moment. Although my hands are so sore, I wash again, in case I have missed a spot and she wants to tell me so. When I have put on my gloves and apron, I take the tray from her to decontaminate. When the water starts flowing from the tap her words begin to pour.

'I've been watching you today and I know you're hurting you take it all on but you can't one day it will catch up with you and crush you you need to tell Rudy to stop stop making tea for everyone because although you are kind they don't appreciate it and will take advantage the doctors especially because they don't know that you're being kind they think it is your job and it isn't they think you are there to put actions to their words but it's much more than that and always double-check Wilf's calculations because he is a baby and he is cocky and if he makes a mistake you will get the blame I want you to protect yourself please and what else is going on with you because you are always late and your hair is a bit of a mess and you don't smell but it's a slippery slope I am always here for you you know that don't you?'

I don't know what to say so I nod. She is kind but confrontational. I feel angry that she waited to tell me in a tiny room, where we are being quiet. I turn to her before opening the door into the cubicle and say I always check the drug calculations, no matter who prescribes. We stare at one another, eyes shining in the dark. Her lips are a perfect line and I know that we will talk more later.

Tracy is huddled in a heap on her bed. She has a blanket wrapped around her. The TV is on, blaring, some loud talk show shouting, she is absorbed, the light bounces off her cheeks, her skin taut and shiny from the earlier deluge of tears. She doesn't turn around when we come in. Jennifer opens her mouth to speak to her but I shake my head and gesture towards the cot where Danny sleeps. She is best left to her grief, whichever shape it takes.

Closer to the cot, Danny's breathing is more audible. He is chugging, his chest is quaking. Jennifer rushes to suction him. I work around her, whilst she expertly assesses him, listening with the stethoscope against his chest, feeling his fingers and toes. I disconnect his old fluid lines and reattach new ones. I check the pain-relief prescription against the programme on the pump. I push the button for a bolus of morphine, I wait to watch his face unscrew and soften, imagining the morphine as a white light working through his veins, wiping out the pain. After a minute or two, he settles. Jennifer changes his nappy whilst I caress his cheeks and coo to soothe. She tells me to stay with him, she is going to speak with Dr Lucas.

I silently, secretly say prayers over him. I am saying goodbye. Just in case. Sadness, coldness, darkness settles in my heart and dries it up like a stone.

Jennifer taps the window and beckons me out of the room. I look at Tracy as I leave, she is unchanged in her pile of tissues and television. I go to her and put my arm around her. I give her shoulder a little squeeze. She looks up at me with watery eyes and nods.

'I'm back in tomorrow night,' I say. 'He's fast asleep now and comfy.' She nods again, opens her mouth but is choked, so she just nods, tears steadily streaming. I give her another little squeeze and go.

The lines in Jennifer's forehead are deep, she is worried.

'The doctors don't seem concerned about his breathing. They said the higher dose of morphine will help. They aren't doing anything further and they don't think it will be long. They said they've explained everything to Mum, does she even know? She's just sitting there watching crap TV.'

'They did. They did explain. I think she's just trying to digest it all. But I didn't think Dr Lucas thought it would happen so quickly.'

'I know you've had a crap day,' she says, 'but can you do one last thing? I need to go and prepare handover. Please can you find the box?'

The box.

The box. I nod and the movement makes my heavy heart drop down into my empty stomach.

'I think it's only fair to prepare the girls coming in on the night shift. They're going to have their work cut out for them. Rudy has been in with Florence all this time, she's been nauseous all afternoon.' She smiles at me with sad eyes. I nod. Nothing to say other than this is all really shit.

I Don't Know Where to Look

The baby next door. I am relieved when I look through the window and see Wilf in the room talking to Dad, who seems to be ignoring him and playing a video game. Wilf comes out as I go in. He waits for the red light in the antechamber to stop flashing. He catches me as I draw breath between my front teeth when the water hits my chapped skin. My *tsssssk* concerns him, he reaches into the basin and takes my hands in his, water still running, spraying his shoes. He doesn't notice. He holds my hands up to the little shred of light falling between the gap in the curtains drawn across the window. The light is all colours, flickering from the video game on the television. The colours make my hands look worse, like they are bleeding, dark fluid pouring from the knuckles. But it's just water, mirroring the gore from the game. I hear the faint sound of erratic gunshots. How can the baby sleep through that?

It's not blood, they're just chapped.

He doesn't say anything but he holds my hands. Careful. Careful.

How does this look?

You are here. You are between his hands and mine. You are the water bubbling between us going hot.

I take my hands away when the water starts spilling over the crooks of my elbows and cascading on to the floor. I look at him and give him a half-smile.

I wait for him to say something, his breath is held, he stands close, like Jennifer did. I feel hot and itchy in the tiny room, in my too-tight polyester. Say something. Tell me I've done wrong. I carry on washing my hands, I scrub and let the skin burn.

'Don't,' he says.

I give a half-laugh. I have to.

'Don't scrub so hard. Your hands are fragile. Your skin is … delicate.'

His words are soft.

'I can take a look later, prescribe something for you to take home. An ointment for night-time.'

He is looking at my face but I keep my head bent and I focus on cleaning between my fingers.

Thank you but what I need is a fucking rest.

I am thinking about you. I picture us sitting up in bed, you rubbing moisturiser on my chapped hands, gently massaging my skin, putting a tiny dollop on my nose and laughing as I wrinkle my nose like a rabbit. I picture you kissing me, coming close with your lips, kissing both of my cheeks, the bristles of your whiskers tickling, putting your nose to my nose and we Eskimo-kiss until the white lotion has melted away. You help me on with cotton gloves, scoop my hair up from under my head as I lie back on the pillow, you fan out my hair behind me and stroke it, running your fingers lightly over my forehead and eyelids. You say, 'Shh, go to sleep,' kissing me deeply once. You turn off the light and sleep on your side with your arms around me.

Wilf moves behind me, to leave. I want him to leave, I feel ashamed. You would hate this. You would hit him. You would be swinging for his honest face once, a while ago. But maybe you would not now. His body is very close, he is careful to keep his hands by his sides. I feel his lips hover, I think they brush my hair. He pauses. Today is not the day to be close to me, I am suddenly conscious that I smell like vomit.

'Tracy was sick earlier,' I say. 'She got me.'

He laughs lightly and says quietly, 'I was going to say you smell like lavender soap and tea.'

'Like an old lady?'

We both laugh and he takes the tension with him when he leaves. I am smiling when I finally get through to see the baby next door.

I Don't Know Where to Look – Part Two

The figure dressed in black is executed at close range. The killer lets go of the controller when he sees me. He has hit the pause button, the screen is frozen and spattered with blood. A sinister heartbeat serves as a backing track for bedtime. Where is the baby?

'Hello again,' I say. I think his name is Paul but I stick with Dad, just in case. 'How is little Buddy today?'

Where is Buddy?

He is on the bed next to Dad, sleeping, uncovered, dummy in, no blankets or pillows around him, he could roll and fall. I tell Dad that he should really have a barrier around him. Dad shrugs and says, 'Do you want to just put him in the cot then?'

'Sure, but don't you want to put him to bed?'

'Nah, he just wakes up and cries when I pick him up.'

He watches me gently lift the baby. I cradle him close and walk him over to the cot. I put him down and he doesn't stir, I tuck a blanket over him and wind up the musical mobile hanging from the rails. 'Twinkle Twinkle' tinkles out, a sweet contrast to the sickening heartbeat. Whilst Buddy sleeps I take a last set of vital signs, I reach into my pocket for my folded sheet of paper and realise it is sick-soaked and still in the pocket of my uniform. I will need to retrieve that for writing up my notes later, I feel my nose wrinkle involuntarily at the thought of the sticky sicky paper. I write the observations on a paper towel and scrunch it up and put it in my pocket.

Dad is eating something salty and cheesy. I can see the orange powder settle in the corners of his lips.

'So, overnight your son will need feeding. We've given slightly less through his tube today so that he should wake up hungry, and this is what the doctors want to see, they want him to try and take bottles so we can take the tube out. It will be much better for him and you'll be able to go home sooner.'

Dad keeps his eyes fixed on his snacks and says, 'Yep. I'll get up with him and feed him.'

'Great. I'm back on shift tomorrow night, so see you then.'

The door closes and the game goes back on, gunfire distorting the tinny nursery rhyme. I see Dad shooting down the twinkling stars.

Do I Have to Believe You

The linen cupboard is the brightest room on the ward. The lights are always on. People come in here to cry. They come here for the comforting heat and scent of freshly washed and pressed linen. The sheets are folded and stacked in great piles. Light bounces off the white, heavenly stacks of patiently waiting neat and tidy ghosts, waiting to unfold.

I come in here not to cry but to find the box. The dark towels are kept on the bottom shelf, hidden away so as not to be used by mistake. When I kneel down and pull out the towels, the box is tucked all the way at the back. I sit cross-legged with the box balanced on my knees. I touch the white lace ribbon which holds the lid in place.

It is dusty. There hasn't been a death for a while.

I untie the ribbon and lift the lid.

The prayer cards are yellowed at the edges where age has eaten away at them. The lettering is still gold and holy.

I unfold the tiny white cotton gown, plain and pure and previously worn. It has the same starched smell of the sheets surrounding me. There is a bonnet with a single white ribbon bow at the front. And two pairs of booties in different sizes. One pair is *very small* and the other pair is *tiny*.

At the bottom of the box there is a pile of lacy doilies. They cover a small white leather-bound bible with wafer-thin pages edged with silver. There is a small crystal flute and a single silk rose.

I put everything back in and tie the ribbon. I drape a little pile of dark towels over my arm and take the box, but I pray on the way back to the nurses' station that the towels won't be needed. I walk slowly. I am bringing a makeshift funeral parlour. The box feels flimsy, the lace is fake, everything worn, I wish we could do better.

I set the box down on the desk next to Jennifer. She is typing up the handover sheet, her brows are raised high with concentration. She touches my wrist as I go to pick up my notes.

'Thank you,' she says, gripping my wrist, typing with one hand.

She looks at the towels. 'Oh.'

I lean towards her and say in a whisper, 'These are the things you don't want to have to run off and look for.'

She nods.

I sit behind her and start to write up my notes. Samantha is hovering above me, watching me write.

'Wow, black towels! What are those for?'

Hairs bristle on my neck as I feel her ponytail swishing, disturbing the air around me.

'They're not black, at least we don't call them black. They are dark towels.'

Jennifer halts her typing, she can hear the irritation in my voice. She picks up the conversation for me, I bend my head and continue writing. My eyes are stinging. Her words are my words and I say them along with her in my head.

The towels are not black. The towels are dark. We have them and we hope we never have to use them. We have them because our patients have a low plate-let count. They could haemorrhage, and rather than let the parents see the bleeding, see sopping saturated soaking-wet red towels, we use the dark ones. The dark towels soak up the blood so you can't see the red.

And I look up and see no red in Samantha's cheeks, her face has drained, she is white and silent.

I Didn't Cry on the Way Home

The room smells of burnt toast, the misery is a dark cloud settled over the kitchen counter. The television is blaring. You are drowning out the world with loud sounds and whisky. The glass is empty on the coffee table. Your feet are up next to it. You are slumped and slumbering, don't hear me come in. Why? Why are you drunk? What are you sad about?

The kitchen is covered in crumbs and smears of butter and jam. There are crumbs of cheese. The oven is not on. There is nothing on the hob except a dirty saucepan. My legs shake and my head throbs. I need to eat.

I pour an inch of orange juice into a glass and drink it. I hope the sugar will help me hold out. There isn't much in the fridge but I try. An onion, some tomatoes, garlic. Nothing else needed. I begin chopping the tomatoes into quarters. I place a wedge in my mouth, the flesh bursts, the juice is delicious and slips down my throat. In a roasting tin I pour olive oil and throw in the tomatoes and slices of onion. I leave the garlic cloves in their little purple jackets. Lots of salt and lots of pepper and more oil, I mix with my hands and wince as the juice of the tomatoes runs between the cracks in my skin. Little red waterways. I turn the oven on high and put the tin in. I boil the kettle for stock. I could lie face down on the kitchen tiles and sleep for the rest of my life, but I must try and stay up, to sleep away some of tomorrow before the night shift.

I lean against the oven and feel the heat on my back. You don't stir. When the vegetables are roasted, I squeeze the garlic cloves out of their skins into a pan, the vegetables and golden juices go in with stock and more pepper. I crane my neck to watch you jump when I blend the soup and the blades crack together, smacking liquid against the glass and shredding flesh. In your mouthy fuzzy drunk-mouthed way you ask me what the fuck am I doing.

I ladle the soup into a bowl and butter the last slice of bread. The last slice, a peace offering, a gesture of care. Or an oversight.

I perch on the sofa next to you with the bowl balanced on my knees. I huddle over it and let the steam rise up and curl over my cheeks, coils of warm comfort. Your eyes are on me. I tear the bread and dip it in the soup. I chew slowly, quietly, the butter melts on my tongue, rich and delicious.

You tell me that if you'd known I was going to cook you wouldn't have eaten so much crap. Your

eyes are big and watery, you are gruff and slurring a
little from sleep and booze.

'If I had known I would have to cook, I would've
stopped for something on the way home. I am starving, I didn't have a lunch break today,' I tell you.

You scoff and tell me I never have a lunch break,
I'm always starving and I'm always tired.

Truth.

I lick the spoon. I try to take a mouthful of soup,
but the bread is stuck, soaks up the hot liquid, stopping up my throat. A rough swallow shifts the lump.
The sound of my swallow is loud, I hear the creaking movement of my jaw, the little fizz in my ear.
You are watching me and it feels worse. You can hear
me slurp. Your eyes are rolling with revulsion. I keep
eating. Fuck it. The hot soup burns but I don't slow
down. The spoon clangs my teeth and I feel you reel-
ing. You grip my wrist as I lead the spoon to my
mouth. Fingers curl tightly and you pull my arm
down. The spoon falls to the floor, a metallic clatter
as drops of soup scatter. Red rain. You are breathing heavily, hand still on my wrist. Pain marks your
face. For a moment I think about putting the bowl
to my lips and drinking it down. But I can't eat, I'll
choke. I want this to be over now. Making you angry
won't help. I turn slowly to look at you, expecting
rage, but when our eyes meet there are tears trailing
down your cheeks, dripping into your beard, little
spitting pitter patters of rain landing on leaves in a

forest. Your grip slackens on my wrist, your hand falls to my lap, knocks the soup, the bowl rocks and then the simmering frustration bubbles, I see it in your fingers as they kick out, fingertips flicking, the bowl flips over, a wave of red, splashing down my leg, up the wall, the bowl is smashed on the floor, red spreading. Spreading. You stand quickly, wipe your face with your sleeve, say quietly that you can't do this any more, that you don't love me any more, and leave the room and close the door.

I sit surveying the sea of soup. A second stream of liquid slicking my skin. At least it's not sick this time. Thankfully we never thought to buy a rug. Thankfully we never replaced the pretend-leather sofa. Thankfully we never made this too much of a home.

I begin by picking up the broken shards of china. I end with three sopping stained tea towels, half a roll of kitchen paper, saturated, sludgy. Fingers stained red. I wish I'd brought home some dark towels to soak up the bloody mess.

Oh, How I Need You Now

You go to bed.

And I don't stick around for this shit.

I wash my face and hands in the bathroom. I brush my teeth and cup my hands and gulp down cold water.

I put on my puffy winter jacket and put keys and money in my pockets. I zip the jacket up to my chin, I catch the skin in the fine teeth and unzip and rub the sting. I open the door and pause. I don't know what I'm doing. I don't know where I'm going. I turn and see you standing there, in the darkness. I didn't hear you opening the bedroom door, I didn't hear you stepping out into the hall. I didn't hear you call my name. I can't make out your face, but you are watching me, probably frowning. Probably glad I'm leaving. Darkness suits you, makes you bigger, makes you harder, makes it easier for me to slam the door.

After today, all I wanted to do was sleep. I have been sucked dry. I am an empty shell. Wind rushes through me, lifts up my crust and carries me along the pavement. I take shelter at a bus stop. A shell within a shell. The wind batters the scratched plastic windows. I watch the cars rolling too fast down the road. Open my eyes wide into the headlights. The light stings. Dash out my eyes forever. I am blind by the time a bus comes. I grope the metal hand-rails to pull myself up to the top deck. I sit with the party people playing music and drinking from plastic bottles. They chuck the bottles under the seats when they are empty, the scrunching crunching plastic sounds electric, they are set for a big night.

We get off the bus close to the river. But I am not with them, they leave me standing on my own as I decide which way to go. I look up. I look up at the cranes in the sky, static arms reaching, revealing red orbs. Clouds grow red like hell. I want to go up there. I wonder what it is like up there. I can't get there. I stagger backwards to see the sky. I stand on my tiptoes, I stretch my neck, stick out my arms. Stretch out into the night. And now I know what I'm look-ing for.

I'm Going to Dance It Away

Nobody in there. There are no bodies to absorb the sound. Nothing to plug the beat. The bouncer on the door is a regular man. He's not big or built or intimidating. He doesn't look at me, doesn't ask for identification. He unhooks the sad stained rope from the rusted metal pole and lets me inside. The music thumps me in the face as I enter the blank space.

Two young girls lean on the bar drinking from frosty champagne flutes. They are chattering and laughing, one girl throws her hand up and does a little wiggle. I wasn't going to have a drink but the bartender steps up and smiles at me and shouts over the music, 'WHAT CAN I GET YOU?'

Vodka and Coke.

WHAT?

VODKA AND COKE.

Why? I've never ordered a vodka and Coke in my life. He puts the glass down on the sticky bar as I put money down on the sticky bar. The ice cubes roll in the bottom of the glass, little amber nuggets that tip up, and the fizz is real, it rolls up my nose as I down it. He watches me as I wipe my mouth with the back of my hand and walk away.

The cold bubbling liquid in my belly makes me want to dance. I walk across the empty dance floor and through swing doors at the other end of the room. I know where these go, I have been here before.

The room on the other side is bristling, bouncing, beats banging out. A line for the ladies' toilets, a line for the cloakroom, a line at the bar, green lines cutting across the ceiling, white lines being cut on top of the black plastic surface of a speaker, the heat and the vibrations make the powder jump, noses down and sweeping, swooping up and ah ah ahhh. They sniff and spin around. They can dance now.

I work my way to the middle of the room, shuffling around people's moves. I begin to swing my arms.

And my legs.

I become fluid with the vibrations in the room. I bump against bodies but I am padded and insulated by my jacket. I throw up my hood and I am disappearing here. Strobe light blisters the room. We inflate in that FLASH. And then we burst and spill over each other.

Grabbing and groping but no one grabs me, I spin around and I keep spinning. I wait for the next strobe my heart pounds my head spins I am the beat I am the beat I am the heartbeat that doesn't come, erratic and swirling and jumping jumping. I dance with my head low, I can't make out feet on the floor but I feel the shuffling so I glide. Gliding through the room, swerving around tangled, twitching bodies. I move towards the walls, I want to watch. But as I move into the darkness I know that I have come too close. The walls are lined with clusters of people, standing all too close together, bunched and touching, glowering like the insides of a pomegranate. Too close. Clustering and sinister. I come too close to the red bodies, no faces, just bubbles swathed in smoke, in coke, in drink.

The music changes to a trippy ripping beat, the strobe stays and I see teeth, white teeth and skulls, bopping and jittering. White knuckles of fists clenched around sticky glasses and sticky bodies and now I'm too hot and too wet and I've got to get out of here.

I go back out through the empty bar. The girl that was wiggling is now writhing against the bartender who has his head buried in her neck. Her friend is puking in the corner.

It All Catches Up to Me

All of my clothes go directly on the floor. I'm standing naked and freezing in the bedroom wondering if I should sleep on the sofa. But it's too late now, I slide into bed next to you. I am shivering cold. I tuck myself around you. You are so warm. And with my arms held to your chest and my nose in the crook of your neck I am home. You are sleepy when you take my hand and press it to your lips. And I am fast asleep when you tell me this is the last time.

I Wait for Her Because Without Her I'm Going to Sink

My skin tightens in the salt water and sunshine. The water is blue, blue, blue, stretching out in front of me forever, an extension of the sky, they are the same thing. The only difference between sky and sea and sea and sky is the golden orb, a perfect bobbing orange. But if I swim towards the shore in the low rippling waves and then turn on to my back and stroke my arms against the silky surface, the dazzling sun is both above me and below me and it doesn't really matter because I am floating floating floating. My sister grabs my hand and says come on! We're going! I turn back again to the shore to see my mother lying on a beach towel on the yellow sand. The towel is enormous and blue-and-white-striped, my mother is tiny in a red swimsuit, her hair is permed and puffed out behind her like a little cloud. She is wearing sunglasses that reflect the sea. I wave and she waves back, a sunburnt arm, pink today, brown tomorrow, the tan lasting forever. I follow my sister as she dives under the waves, she is graceful and fast and soon catches up with my father.

He is happiest now.

In the water he is transformed, tanned, not tired, smiling, not shouting. He dunks his head under, rises and slicks back his hair. Let's swim out further, girls, but keep close. I match my sister's stroke, arms flying through the water. Father is farther, we follow, flinging our arms out, sending cuts across waves ripping. We splash, water is everywhere, in my eyes, in my mouth, I dive under and rise into the sun. I push the water and breath out of my nose, pinch my nostrils and wash away the snot and salt from my fingertips. I wipe my eyes and draw my hair back from my forehead. Father's feet flip in and out of the water, I reach for them. My sister is laughing, joy and freedom pouring from her, swimming, singing, sun-tingling, she touches the shimmering rays of light on the water, she catches them in her cupped hands, little silver fishes, she throws them high into the sky. Diamonds shower us. We swim on. Into the blue. Deeper and deeper. Further. Following. Father signals us to swim under the wave about to break over us, we duck down, resurface, laughter sprinkles from our mouths, mingles with popping and zinging of dissolving sea foam. We duck down again for the next wave and the next and the next. When we rise the air feels cooler than before. The water is darker.

The sun is still shining but it is higher now. Father is still smiling, still swimming, but the next wave that comes is bigger, he doesn't dive fast enough, he gets caught in the crest. Arms flail and foam flies. The sea spits him back out, he splutters, he is shocked. My sister laughs.

We settle on the surface, treading through the troughs when they come, bobbing like seagulls, playing it cool. I look back at the shore, I can just make out the golden band of sand in the distance, a tiny speck that could be Mother, could be the salt fizzing my eyes, the glare of the sun, could just be a speck. I turn to my sister. But she is not there. I meet a wall of water.

Slammed. Slapped. There is no splash, the force is too great. I feel my muscles strain to hold on. But hold on, there is nothing to hold on to. I am under. My muscles strain, my bones are bolsters, tissue tightens to stay fixed to my skin. Pushed down and held under by the weight of the water and raging waves. I push back, arms thrashing, but I am held tightly and I'm tired, so tired. My lungs burn to breathe. I try to look up, to see the surface, but I'm so far down, there is not much light, there is dark water, heavy as cement. I shut my eyes. What can I do now? Behind my eyes there is darkness too. And specks. Hundreds of tiny specks. They are red, they could be my mother, on the sand, waving goodbye, waving goodbye. My battered arms wave back limply.

I am dizzy and I am dying.

The specks become bigger, they bleed into each other, until the specks become drops and the drops become pools and the pools become lakes and the lakes become seas until all I can see is darkness.

A sharp pinch pulls at the skin on my shoulder, pulls me out of the water. The pinch is painful, I touch the fingers that pull the flesh from the blade of bone, I grip the wrist, wringing the wet skin. The arm is my sister's saving me from drowning, I surface to the sound of my father screaming.

I wake up with the pain of the pinch still present. I gasp at the feel of the cold flesh still in my grasp. My fingers are hooked around a wrist of brittle bones, skin so thin it is there and it is not there, I touch the bone, so cold it numbs my fingertips, and I lose the grip, the wrist belongs to no arm and no one.

But someone. There is someone.

I open my eyes, looking for him, the anger approaching my lips even though I know he is not there, the bed is empty. He is long gone.

But there is someone.

Milky light seeps through the slats of the blinds. My eyes are blurry, still full of sleep and specks and seawater. I can't see. But I can feel. I sense someone next to the bed, standing over me, sense the silence about to be broken, the mouth falling open, the breath bubbling, boiling, coiling up through slackened lungs, sacs unused and clogged with dust, a wheezing whistle tipping the air. I listen for the breath but I only hear my own, shallow from the night of sea swimming, slowing now, stopped up with fear. If someone is there, why don't they speak, why don't they breathe? Am I imagining the cold fleshy fingers, the pinch that lingers?

I am too scared to look so I thrust out my arm, spread my fingers into the empty air, dashing away the demon that isn't there. The emptiness is a chasm that I cannot consider right now. I reach for sleep. And sleep comes in waves, I let them wash over me, with each one I reach out for hands to hold, my father pulling me back into the water, my sister pulling me out. I stretch my fingers to feel theirs but they drift away, they drift away, as they have drifted away.

I Didn't Drown

This time when I wake, the light in the room is brighter, the day is older. The image imprinted in my mind is the blue-and-white-striped towel from my dream, draped across my vision like a flag. This is a stock image. This is how I know I was dreaming. The towel in real life is small, flimsy, flutters in the breeze blowing up sand, spreading sprinkles everywhere, sand landing in unwanted places. My sister and I had matching towels, bright red, blue and yellow, a primary beach scene, a sun, a sea, a bucket and spade, wrapping round and round and round us when our bodies were small, the softness of the towel tickling sun-kissed areas, chafing chapped sandy bottoms. But as we grew, they did not, we sat on them for as long as we could. And then they became towels for hair dyeing at home. My mother's soft brown perm became woven with white. She would sigh loudly with each sighting of a new silver streak. And every few weeks she would stand at the bathroom sink, staring in the mirror, dolloping dye on to her head, piling her hair high, scooping and swirling her hair up foamy and creamy. She'd call out to me for the towel to be passed, I'd press it on her shoulders, she was a whipped-cream queen.

A catalogue of her dyeing. The towels were marked with the colours of her years. At first, dark chocolate, milk chocolate, redder to mahogany, mouse brown, BLONDE. Washed out by white, she admitted defeat. Blonde at her age? The time came to be gracefully grey. We called it silver. The hair stripped of its thickness by the chemical fix. Thin on top, threadbare like the ancient towels. But not dead yet. The towels live on, a third life in the rags hanging in my father's shed.

I can smell the oil on the rags. I can see my father sitting in the car, he says pass me the rag, Laura, I can't see a bloody thing. And he wipes the windscreen vigorously, the rag is thrown into my lap, soaked in condensation. He is hunched, leaning close to the wheel, eyes squinting and fixed to the road. Worry rolls over his face, skin withering. Headlamps of oncoming cars flash and wash his face in stark white light, highlighting the creases so deep where the worry beds down and keeps his eyes tightly open at night. Lack of sleep leaks from him. His body is low and slow, every move made smaller and smaller as he shrinks into endless days. We ride side by side somewhere, his endless day, my endless night, our exhausted breath fogging up the windows until we can't see each other any more and we can't see anything in front of us.

So with that sad thought I drag my sorry ass out of bed.

I have never felt so empty. I should be thin from barely eating, from working shifts without stopping for a drink, for grabbing a bite, a literal bite. The uneaten food still finds a way to punish me. I stretch my tired arms and legs, I grab the layer of fat that still sits around my empty belly. I squeeze it and breathe in and I look in the mirror and say to myself I look thin like this and then let go of my gut and watch the wobble and say maybe this is why you don't love me any more?

I will never know because I will not ask you.

I walk into the kitchen and fill a glass of water and drink it down. The floor is sticky from the spilled soup and I set to scrubbing it in my pyjamas. My empty stomach is the soundtrack to my chores. The rumbling grumbling echoes over the sound of sweeping, swiping dust from surfaces, drumming away as I scratch at the grit and grime on the kitchen counter. I puff up pillows and fold clothes. Your clothes and mine. Everything together now for the last time. When I put your socks in the washing basket, I say out loud I will not miss this. The things I will not miss make a bigger list than things I will. I will miss your arms. I will miss the warmth of your body in the bed. There is a little soft patch of skin on the back of your neck that I like to touch. I will miss that. I will miss the lick you give your lips before you speak but I won't miss the words that follow and fall out of that wry wet mouth.

I take my pyjamas off, now sweaty and soaked with soap suds. As the top goes over my head I get a whiff of the dusty plastic vacuum smell. I dress in leggings and a sports bra. I put on your favourite T-shirt which is creased and dirty but still feels forbidden. I brush my greasy hair into a ponytail which doesn't need pins to stay in place. This run should be easier with nothing inside me. I should be light as air. I should be fucking floating.

I Fear

Galloping manic. Heart pounding, hair flying, my feet slam the path, reverberations travel through my bones, up and rumbling in my ears, the vibrations make my back teeth shake and knock together, I try to keep my tongue out of the way. This is the way to run. Skeleton quaking, lungs bursting, everything everything everything hurting. Each step is a stamp, an essential connection with concrete, crushing that empty feeling. I am here. Solid, steadily moving through the world. I can be alone. I can be a force. I don't need half-love, half-life, half is not enough. I can be whole with nothing. I came from nothing. I came from nowhere. I can be anywhere now, without. Here I am without. But here I am. Flying.

My thoughts unravel like ribbons as I rush through the trees. They are long and are tied to the tips of my fingers, they blow in the breeze, I air them out. I am careful not to let them catch on twigs and leaves. They stream out, all colours and rippling noise, and then I let them go. I untie the pain and sadness, I scatter it amongst the fallen leaves and dirt. I push myself to keep going, to move the muscles, to blow out the air that was breath before and is used up and no good any more. I push, push, push to move and think and function, the collapse will have to come later.

Afternoon sunlight saturates the canopy of leaves, spreading like sacred water, golden and green, pouring on to the path. The light lifts me, I move faster. The air is cool and fresh on my face. The trees and shrubs blur into mossy green messes, the golden light is glittering on crusted bronze and brown leaves. I let myself smile a little as I skip over stones, branches brushing my hair and –

A cry rises, I am surprised by the sound, it emerges, bursts from my own gaping mouth. Slam, sickening whack, crack. My head rolls forward with force. Searing pain and shock makes me stop.

Thwack.

I am hit.

I am hurt.

A brick. A hammer. A dagger.

Dazed. Head lolling forward. Rolling around, heavy, barely hanging on to my weak neck.

The air behind me is disturbed, I feel it spreading, I feel it pressing in. I will my wobbly legs to run on. I shuffle along the path. Crack. WHACK. Scrappy scraping nail through skin through skull dragging drawing open I am shrieking, screaming, running for

my life, scrabbling my way through the brush screaming, eyes streaming. I feel the air ripping open above
me behind me I see the enormous shadow of splayed
wings the thing is following me flying, swooping
down snatching at my hair, reaching deep with claws,
beak breaking skin, driving down digging for bone.
I snatch breaths between screams hoping someone
hears. Wings thrash behind me, I see black-feathered
blurs. Another spear of pain dragging across my scalp,
I flip my head back and forth to fight it off. Running
don't stumble it'll go for your eyes. I bring my
clenched fists up close to my face. Please, someone.
Barking breaks through my hoarse shrieking, I see a
dog up ahead and I run towards it, I rush out into a
clearing, a woman is coming to me with her arms
open. She commands her dog: 'SCOUT!' she shouts.
He is barking, raging, hind legs bent he is ready to
bounce, bound up the tree trunk. The woman has
worked her arm around my shoulders, she is shhhing
and soothing me and I am cowering. The crow settles
on a high branch. He is watching me. He is fucking
huge. I point to it. The woman is dismayed.

'I thought you were being murdered,' she says.

I thought I was being murdered.

'You're bleeding.' She looks at the blood I have
dripped on her shoulder. I put my hand to my head.
My hair is wet, my hand is red.

'Oh, I'm so sorry.' I step a little way from her but
I'm shaking, she grasps my arm.

94

'It's okay, come with me, I'll help you back to the canal.'

The black crow sits, waiting, watching, feathers glistening in the lowering light. I can't make out its eyes, but I feel it watching me. Every bit of it is shining.

Scout gives a final growl and follows us. The woman holds my arm firmly until we reach the cobbled path.

'Thank you,' I say, snivelling, wiping my wet face with the back of my hand.

'No problem, you're sure you'll be okay?'

'Yes, thanks again.' I turn towards home, she stands and waits and watches me a little way.

Every step I take is slow and scared. I keep my hand pressed to the wound, my bloody wet hair dries quickly and sticks to my skin. I sob all the way. People go by with curious and pitying eyes. No one stops, but I'm glad, I won't be able to get the words out.

The sun is setting, a big round yellow egg yolk, forked open and flowing, the last of the sunlight running into the murky canal, darkness dissolving the day. The signal of my start. I want to start again. What has happened? What is happening? Ghastly ghostly darkness flocking in on black wings.

If I told you, you would laugh.

Who gets attacked by a crow?

This would only happen to Laura.

I shiver and shake my way home and into the shower, power up the heat and pressure. My head stings as the water hits, rushing down, pinkish.

I comb my wet hair and wait for the steam on the mirror to disappear. My reflection is misted, faded. I am not there, I am not here. The mist in the mirror drifts. The bathroom is full of fog, I feel the fullness and could there be someone else? I am truly spooked, goose-pimpled full of fear from creepy water-logged dreams, the wet slithering arm on my shoulder, the murderous crow.

I pull the towel tightly around me, I wipe the mirror, my skin squeaks as I streak the glass. My face, my sad face, is not mine but some other person's. Drawn and grey. My lip curls up, a rasping gasp of horror escapes from me, I whip around and face the face but the face is just fog flurrying. I open the door and it escapes. The mirror clears and I tilt my head to see the wound, I part my hair, my scalp is scored in places, the skin is red and raw with scratches. Bleeding begins again but it is insignificant. Leaning over the basin, I begin to feel pain in my stomach, a gurgling pain, an empty belly, gassy and growling.

I feel stupid, I feel shitty, I feel starving. I stalk to the kitchen shaking myself off. And I put the kettle on to boil eggs.

I Function

I feel better with a belly full of milky tea and eggs. When I remembered we were breadless, I softened the hard edge of anger sticking in my throat with furry, slowly moulding raspberries and thick yoghurt.

My head is tender, my brain feels like tenderised beefsteak simmering in juices. I take pain killers and wear my hair loose. I find myself standing outside the hospital and wonder how I got here. My backpack has a clean uniform, clean socks and snacks inside. I brought a book to read on my break. I am partly impressed and partly terrified at my ability to function, to pull myself together, to remain present and to present myself. I am half an hour early.

We will all be here early tonight. We all want to know. Poor Danny, what has happened to you? He has been with us so long, he has made us all little-bit mothers, little-bit fathers. And when I peer inside the doctor's office and see Wilf sitting at Dr Lucas's desk with his head in his hands, I know for sure and my heart stings. He is surrounded by papers and stacks of notes, blood results and scan reports, meaning what now? Numbers adding up to exactly nothing.

His hair is sticking up. He takes his spectacles off and rubs his eyes with his fists. And then he slams a fist down on the desk and the papers jump and I jump. I have never seen him in emotion, he is always steady. Then he is calm, he reaches for his mug and puts it to his lips. He frowns when he tips it for liquid and nothing comes, realises it is empty, but he holds on to it. His face in concentration is sort of handsome. I could watch all day, I could stand on the edge of his life, but maybe I want to say, maybe I want to say something, and I disturb him by pushing the door open and the squeaking startles him and he drops his mug. It bounces on the carpet and I rush forward to catch it. I see stars when I straighten back up. I place the mug down and grip the desk with both hands, knuckles showing white as the bone beneath the skin.

'Are you all right, Laura?'

'He's gone, isn't he?'

He nods.

'When?'

'This morning, just after five. He stopped breathing.'

He stopped.

'Tracy held him. Her parents came right away. Dr Lucas has been with them for most of the day, he left the ward to see his other patients and hasn't made it back yet. I'm bringing together the last lab results and notes to make sure everything is in order. I don't want him to come in tomorrow to deal with chaos. Tracy has gone home with her parents. She was clinging to the doorframe.'

And I can see her, hanging on, long pale fingers snatching at the doorframe, gripping until her yellowed fingernails turn white and the blood cells in her nail beds begin to burst, gripping, grasping, holding on. Until the world stops. She will always be here and she will never leave him. Holding on. Holding.

Was she grasping at my wrist somewhere in my dream, was she screaming? Pity floods and sinks my insides. No one should have to see their child die.

Are you okay? He's asking me and I'm asking him and I tell him the strangest thing has happened today, I tell him about the crow.

He brings a chair over and folds me into it. He swings around to face me, his knees are almost touching mine. I tell him about the crow. His lips are drawn straight, two thin pink lines. His eyes grow wide and round as I tell him about the drilling beak and enormous wings, his brow has more furrows than ever before. I tell him I took a shower. I tell him I have eaten. When I finish speaking I meet his eyes fully and we are fixed for a long, slow moment. And then he cracks. His laugh is low and throaty. His eyes are glistening, glazed with tears as if I have tickled him. I watch him fold and unfold, his abdomen is an accordion, pushing out long notes of laughter.

He puts his hand over his mouth to quieten himself. His cheeks are flushed.

'I'm sorry, you poor thing. But that is the strangest and funniest thing I've ever heard. Are you all right? Let me take a look. I think you're going to need a tetanus injection.'

He stands and steps behind me. Without asking, he places both hands on my shoulders. He brings his face close to my head, I feel his breath on my flesh; the open, sensitive skin tingles at the lightest touch of air.

'I'm sorry I laughed. This wound looks quite sore. I'll clean it for you and go down to the pharmacy and see if they have any vaccinations in stock.'

He is already out of the door as I say thanks quietly. I go to the staffroom for a glass of water. The rest of the night staff haven't arrived yet. I glance up at the rota stuck to the fridge door with chipped souvenir magnets. Ancient faded fish and cocktail glasses. The fish has lost its goggly eyes. It swims blindly and I know how it feels. I look at the rota lines crawling incoherently around the page, long days into long, long nights, weekends whenever, annual leave dotted with smiley faces, lucky people going to sunny places, and cross-cover crossings out, cross lines that don't match up, will you cover my night shift because I can't work three in a row, I have children, don't you know? I can't give chemotherapy, I am not competent to look after tracheostomy patients, I have no patience left with the family in room 7, I've looked after them every shift, and please can you work next Saturday, someone is off sick, someone's mother is coming to visit, someone has theatre tickets. I always say yes. To be useful and hoping that one day, when I need to swap a shift or when I need time off, someone will say yes to me. But nothing is ever pressing.

I trace my rota line with my fingertip. It is erratic. It is antisocial. It doesn't really matter any more. Without you, I have nowhere I need to be. I think about the letter I need to write later to Matron, to request a room in the nurses' home. I don't want to live in a single-bedded room with a hob and a sink. But you will stay in the flat. You have the money. What do I have? The split is raw, like my skin has been unzipped and my chest is open, my heart climbs up and clambers out on aortic arms, dragging ventricles and veins, squeezed dry, old, blue and used. My lonely lungs will continue to breathe. Blood will make its own way to where it needs to be. I will live without the thumping beat, the throbbing beast, it belongs to you now, for a while at least. Please send it back, half full, with no hard feelings.

Wilf returns to wash out the wound and fill the void. I am grateful he hasn't tried to send me to Accident and Emergency. He is taking his time, his own time, his shift should have finished an hour ago.

He pulls me into the treatment room, he tries to help me up on to the couch and I clumsily decline and kick him in the shin. He shakes his head and says don't worry. He pulls paper towels out of the dispenser and tucks them in the neck of my shirt.

'I'll try not to soak you,' he says. He washes his hands, taking time over the creases between his fingers, he washes up to his elbows like he is scrubbing to perform surgery, he is lost in the motions. He pours little sachets of pink antiseptic into a plastic bowl and drops sterile gauze into the liquid. He pulls on purple gloves and rests the bowl on the couch next to me. He squeezes the gauze, the liquid tinkles in the bowl. He stands in front of me, leaning in to dab the wound. My face is close to his chest. I can't help breathing in a little bit of him. The top two buttons of his shirt are undone, a sprinkling of fine, coppery hairs curl over pale skin, glistening with moisture. He is slightly sweaty but his scent is not unpleasant. Defining the scent is dangerous. I will covet it, try to replicate it, wrongly crave it when comfort is all I wish for. He dabs gently, but the drips still sting and tingle. Cells shifting, invisible knitting, but I feel them creeping over my skull covering it like a cap. A drop of antiseptic dribbles down the side of my face, a pink tear from the pink fleshy tear. Wilf brings a gloved finger to my cheek to catch it, I look up at him, he looks down at me, touching my face, and then the real tears come. I weep into his chest.

Shoulders shrugging, uncontrollable shuddering. He peels his gloves off and puts his arms around me. His fingers find their way to the nape of my neck, he strokes my skin gently. He lets me let it all out.

His wet shirt clings to my cheek. He waits for me to speak. But nothing comes. I don't know what to tell him. I'm a mess, my life is a mess, he knows already because we share this space where we are always on hold and are always on call. We are cotton buds sucking up the sadness of others, we are saturated, we are saviours. We absorb pain, too thick with mess to notice that everything around us is drying up and growing over. We will wake up one day in a wasteland, surrounded by the crumbling bones of those who loved us and waited for us to love them back. We did not forget but we were too busy being useful. We will crumble next to them but it will take forever, we will sit amongst the piles of dust alone.

When I have finished shucking out my sorrow on to his shirt, he steps away to prepare the tetanus vaccine. I roll up my sleeve. He says nothing but looks me in my sore red eyes. I see redness around his too. He might have been crying. He wipes the top of my arm with an alcohol wipe, one swift swipe, he pinches my skin, puts the needle in, I feel the liquid push, the rush, the needle slip out and plaster patch.

'Thank you for helping me,' I say. I smile feebly at him.

'It's my pleasure. Your arm will ache for the next few days, your wound will heal quickly.'

He reaches out his hand and it hovers above my head. For a moment I think he is going to ruffle my hair, but his hand remains still and he says through a smile, 'Perhaps the crow was jealous of your glossy plumage.' His finger drifts down towards my shoulder like a feather, he grasps a lock of hair between his thumb and forefinger, he gently smooths out the ends and drops it.

'You need to go home,' I say.

He nods and rubs his eyes with clenched fists, he stretches, his head nearly touches the ceiling.

'I'm back tomorrow night; you're on too, right?'

'Yes,' I say.

Tomorrow night and forever.

He says goodbye and leaves me in the treatment room, damp and sore and sad.

I shuffle off the examination couch and go to get changed.

I'm Not in Charge

Rudy is in charge and the night is quiet. Florence is poorly and keeping him busy. He laughed when I told him about the crow, but when I told him about the break-up he hugged me and went easy on me and only allocated me Buddy.

Everyone feels the loss. Everyone is quiet and careful, more careful than usual, to check the safety equipment, to double-check the medications, to watch their patients, eyes open, eyeing everything. I speak to Dad at the start of the shift and ask him not to play video games tonight, for peace and quiet. He nods, says of course, says poor little chap, his mother must be in bits. I warm to him a little bit, but he still doesn't hold his baby, still doesn't respond to his gurgles and giggles. I dim the lights in the room, the baby is settled and dozing in the cot, the television stays on and Dad is transfixed, staring at the muted scenes of a detective film. I leave them in their own kind of peace.

I peer into the window of Danny's room. Danny's old room. The only light in the room bleeds through the half-drawn blind, rusty red glowing from the street lamp below. The cot has been stripped and cleaned, Tracy's things are packed, the suitcase stands in the middle of the room. And soon it will be gone, the cot will be made up with clean, crisp white sheets and a new baby will appear, fresh sickness, old sadness, the cycle will begin again and everyone will try harder than ever.

At midnight Rudy asks me to order pizza, he'll pay, he says, so I call from the staffroom and everyone is ravenous. When it arrives, I offer to watch the ward whilst the others go and eat, but Rudy puts his arm around me and says absolutely not, Amir will stay with the patients and he really doesn't mind if we take a break first.

The box is damp and hot in my hands, I lift the lid and the smell of melted cheese overwhelms my nostrils, I almost dribble, my stomach sings to be fed.

'Thank goodness we went large! Twice!' says Rudy, he grabs a slice and ploughs it straight in his mouth. He shuts his eyes and chews quickly, cheese dangling, little strings stitching his lips together. I take smaller bites, enjoying the sharp tomato sauce on my tongue and the slightly chewy, slightly crispy crust between my teeth. My belly warms with the first slice, the second slice slips down quicker, tomato and cheese, everything on my chin, I don't care, I wash it all down with strong coffee and I am satisfied.

'Thanks, Rudy, that was good.'

We take more coffees back to the ward. I place both our mugs beside the computer and put my hand on Amir's shoulder.

'You're up,' I say. 'Don't worry, there's plenty left.'

I wander up the corridor to check on my patient. I peer through the window. He is curled in his cot, the blanket is spread over his rump, slightly sticking up in the air. I can see his chest rise and fall, his little cheeks puffed in pure rest, sweet abandon, his pink lips in a perfect pout. To sleep so deeply – it warms me to see rest reviving the imperfect body. My eyes move across the room. Dad is sitting in the chair, with his head bent down. The glow from the grainy film casts only dim light, I see him in silhouette, he is bending forward, his black-hooded jacket pulled up over his head. At first he looks like he is slumped forward, sleeping, but then the slight movements of his arms show he is tying his shoes, I think he is tying his shoes, or leaning over to reach for something that has fallen to the floor.

He's a strange guy.

I turn away from the window. I am stunned. The pizza in my stomach starts sliding back up my gullet. Dad is walking towards me, in a red jacket, hands jammed in his pockets, wrapped in ghostly blue wisps of cigarette smoke. I whirl around, looking back through the window, pivoting on hollow wobbling legs.

The chair is empty.

I press my face up against the glass, squinting into the darkness. The chair is completely empty. Light from the television streaks the wipe-clean vinyl cushion. Ghastly glowing green. Not black, not full of shape, not a form, leaning forward, face in shadow. Not Dad, not who I thought. My phantom heartbeat thuds in my ears. There was someone in the room. There was someone in that chair. And if they are no longer sitting there then they must still be in the room, in the corner, in the darkness. The baby sleeps on undisturbed.

I rush into the antechamber and scrub my hands quickly, I throw on an apron. My hands aren't properly dry, my grip slips on the door handle, I let the door slam shut. The doorframe shakes. I rush over to the cot, the baby has raised his hands in tiny fists to his face, but still sleeps soundly with little snores escaping every other breath. I don't want to turn on the lights, they will be too bright. I pull my pen-torch out of my pocket and press and hold the button down with my thumb. I swipe the air, arm outstretched, throwing a pathetic glow into the corners of the room. I tiptoe behind the cot and reach out into the darkest corner, the weak yellow light shaking in my trembling hand. My plastic apron crunches and rustles with every movement. Light falls on precisely nothing. But I knew already. There is no one here. I am creeping around like a pathetic plastic-coated ninja. I laugh quietly. I am losing my mind. When I entered the room, I knew. I could sense the baby, smell his sweetness, feel the warmth of his rest. The room is small, small enough to feel the closeness of others, and I cannot feel anyone here. I can feel his father, I can smell his father, removing his smoky, damp jacket, pumping soap on to his hands, trying hard to leave the outside outside. But I saw someone sitting in the chair and I felt it. I felt sure of it. Tiredness is playing tricks and I'm tired of it now.

I Have to Believe That It Is

The ward is empty and silent. I try to sit for a moment at the nurses' station but I'm too scared. I wait outside the antechamber where Rudy is washing his hands. When he comes out I tell him about the figure in the chair, about the black hood, the darkness. When we pass the baby's room we stop and look through the window. Staring at the empty chair, he tells me he's seen it too.

The darkness?

No.

The figure.

The ghost.

Ridiculous.

Nonsense.

No no, it's true.

You are so full of shit.

He laughs. I give him a shove.

I'm so tired. I rub my eyes hard.

'I don't appreciate you winding me up when weird and bad things have happened to me today.'

'I know, I know, I'm sorry.' He rubs my shoulder.

'Jennifer is crazy. Don't tell her what you saw, she'll be all over you! She sees ghosts every shift in this place.' He smirks and shakes his head. 'Can you do me a favour? I need to take blood from Florence and would really like to be able to hand over the results in the morning so Dr Lucas can make a decision on her antibiotics. Please can you run the samples up to the lab?'

You have got to be kidding.

But he's not. He's the nurse in charge tonight and he hands me the samples and holds the door open for me.

I Follow the Footsteps

The windows reflect the white walls and my white face, stark, strobe-like against my electric-blue uniform. I am a bluebottle fly buzzing inside a strip light. I move quickly along the corridor, I don't like not being able to see outside, not seeing the night. The reflections are endless, like there is no world outside and there is only whiteness and sickness inside. At the end of the corridor is a heavy blue shiny door, with smooth shiny yellow acrylic handles. The colours are a small attempt at cheerfulness, but nobody notices. The doors open and the children don't notice, the parents don't notice, they are pulled into the white tunnel and there they stay.

I pull the door open.

A cool empty space. A cold empty silence. I realise that I have been hot all night, roasting red-faced, not thinking straight. This corridor is creepy like the tunnel but for a different reason. My footsteps echo. The huge glass windows sit loosely in peeling wood-panelled walls. The glass shakes, close to breaking, beaten by the wind, high and whistling. The shell of the hospital is crumbling, but they won't tear it down. There is too much history here. I pass stones laid by lords and princes marking donations of ancient millions. I open another door, old and oak, that leads to the laboratory. I say hello to the domestic who is furiously mopping the floor, slopping water and suds over a black mark on the tiles. He nods and pauses whilst I tiptoe over the soapy puddle. I open another door and hear 'Mind you don't slip on the wet floor' as it closes. I begin climbing the stairs to the sixth floor. The walls are washed in dirty beige, newly painted, the smell is still strong, I touch the wall and it is dry but slightly sticky. As I reach the second floor I see a sign for the nurses' home, the inside entrance to my new flat. I think about how good it will feel to be able to collapse into bed so soon after a shift. Living here might not be so bad.

I trudge up the third and fourth flights of stairs, the silence of the stairwell is broken by my breathlessness and the pounding of my pulses pushing blood around, rushing around, powering my tired legs. I grip the banister and drag my hand over the smooth wood, worn down by many hands, sanded down by sand-paper skin. The banister creaks as I rest my weight on it and catch my breath. I lean my head back into the open column of space, the air flows coolly from the ground up, and I look up to the ceiling of old wooden beams and cobwebs. I see blackness. Moving.

I hear something brushing against the metal railing and see long fingers trailing over the banister two floors above me. Footsteps echo that aren't my own.

'Hello?'

Shoes clack on the tread, tapping up the steps. Steps fall slowly. The fingertips barely touch the wood, the blackness is a long dress trailing.

'Hello?' I call again. The footsteps stop. The black fabric swishes with the sudden cease of movement. I run up the steps, keeping my eyes fixed upwards. The footsteps fall again, faster this time, but not as fast as mine. I rush, my sides brushing the banister, my hip hits the turn in the wood and sends a shooting pain across my pelvis. I yelp and it echoes and I listen to the bouncing sound bumping over the footsteps and then there are just my footsteps, the others have stopped. I hang over the banister and look up and there's no one there. No trace of the fingertips, no fluttering black fabric. But there was someone there. I bite my lip and say fuck out loud. I want to see her. I want to know who she is. I breathe deeply and climb the last few steps to the lab. I look up one last time and I see her.

She is flying.

She is falling.

Her face is contorted, terror flows out of her mouth, a spewing scream, it splashes up the walls as she falls, her face passes mine and I see the whites of her eyes shot through with red bursting blood vessels and tears streaming from pits of sleeplessness. Her skin is grey and flaking, her face is eroding. Her long black dress blows up and out like steam-engine smoke. I am frozen to the spot and I draw in breath and shut my eyes waiting for the sound of her smashing on to the floor. I hold my breath for what feels like forever but the sound never comes.

The Moment I Didn't Want to Share With You

Out on the other side, out of night, rays of the rising sun draw the new day. The morning warms my chilled bones. My head is full of fog, my mouth is fuzzy. I desperately want to brush my teeth my tongue is dry and sticking I have that sicky feeling. I keep my head up, concentrate. Try to stay awake. Desperation drags me across the city. I meet the sleepiness of others but I will not be tempted by them. They are gluttons, they have had their fill of full night's sleep. How dare they dare to dream extra dreams in front of me? They are the enemy and I am in their territory. They close their eyes and nod their heads as the train carriage rocks through dark tunnels. They yawn. I look away and hold my head up with both hands.

I am so close now. I might just make it. So close to home, to bed. I picture myself peeling back the sheets.

So close. And there you are. You are walking towards me. You look shrunken and crumpled. You are walking quickly and, as you approach me, I think for a moment that you might not stop. And you don't stop, you keep walking past me, you pretend you don't see me, you don't look at me but I look at you, your tired eyes, red, like you've been crying. You keep going, but I am stuck, stopped, choked. I watch you walking with your head down, big bag slung over your shoulder. Going somewhere. Going to stay somewhere, with someone, who?

You didn't stop.

I want to cry out.

Don't unravel. Not here, not in the street.

In the bedroom, in the dark, I button up my pyjamas and climb into bed. I bury my face in the pillow and spend some time untying the knots in my chest, I release these damn tears, they flow into the pillow and I weep myself to sleep.

I Thought I Would Be a Day Sleeper

This time we are bone dry. We are standing on the
balcony of a concrete high-rise. There is a sheet of
thick glass behind us, a wall that comes to our waists
in front of us, there is no moon in the night sky, no
relief of a breeze, there is nowhere to go but over
the wall and down. The view of the city is brutal.
Buildings rise out of blackness, terrible grey grave-
stones of the godless, bleeding open mouths of watery
shining windows. Empty windows. No signs of life.
We are here. The woman is standing next to me. She
is still. Her heart is still. And mine is too. And mine
is too. Her hair is pulled away from her pale face.
She stares straight ahead. Her dress is long and black,
heavy skirts cover her feet. She might not have feet.

She floats.

I turn to her to speak, but my mouth is sewn shut.
I am toothless and gummy, tongue dry and curled
up, stuck to the roof of my mouth. I try to stretch

my arms out to her but I have no arms. Limbless. A disconnected brainstem. A stump.

Veins track across her temple, twisting grey vines over her face, they grow from her, writhing in the air, weaving a child's game of cat's cradle between us. Veins wind around my shapeless face and then we are connected. We are tethered. We share the same headache. We share the same wake.

We stand in stillness. We stand in agony.

She knows that I cannot bear to stand any longer. She floats towards the wall. Before she throws herself off, she turns to look at me. Her eye sockets are empty, there are two huge gaping black holes and, as she falls over the wall, I fall into the black burning holes. I hear the crack as she hits the concrete, the street splits, my head splits, pain rakes open my brain. We are both scattered, splattered on the ground.

I Can't Find a Light on Anywhere

I wake up in another day, or is it the same? I look at the clock and see I have only been asleep for a few hours. I cram my eyes shut and try, try, try to sleep again but my mind resists. My exhausted body aches, my head thumps, my fingers settle on a lump that has grown through the night, I should get some ice but my body can't move, won't move. I settle on the cold side of the pillow for soothing.

I still see the face, the black holes and the mouth gaping open, withered lips but not from age. The woman in my dream was young, but rotten. She was lying at the bottom of the lake in the same strange billowing black dress. She was standing on the Tube platform, she was praying in the chapel, she was sitting in the chair, she fell from the top of the stairwell. I remember her. I feel her. But I don't know who she is. I am cold and shaking, I pull the quilt tightly around my body.

I am scared.

It is strange to dream. So I don't. I drift, I shudder, I drift, I shudder, I drift I shudder I do this for hours until I am shuddering shuddering, the walls shake, I am not fully awake, the phone is ringing ringing in sleep in real life, blood rises when I rise, walk, sleep-walking. Waking.

'Hello, Laura?'

Speaking.

'It's Oliver from the hospital residences service. We've got a room available, it's just been vacated. Can you come and see it today? If you don't want it, someone else will. Can you come at six?'

I feel like I'll never sleep again. I take the phone back into bed with me. I burrow under the blankets and call my mother. I talk to her in the darkness with the blankets over my head. I cry a little. I stay under the blankets until my breath has fogged the air and turns my skin wet and wrinkly. I emerge. I breathe. I listen whilst my mother tells me it'll be okay. She tells me you are a complete shit. I laugh and she laughs. I nod when she says it's probably for the best. She tells me I need a break and that I should come home after my night shifts and she's right and I will, I have three days off. Just one more night. I tell her I will see her tomorrow and hang up the phone.

Do You Feel as Lonely as I Do

Oliver's smile is wide but not warm. I'm late and he's waiting to go home. He's polite and holds the door open for me. I peer into the dark room, he reaches behind me and flicks the switch on the wall. The single bulb flickers and slowly illuminates my new home. I step into the small space which smells like bleach. It's clean, at least. The blinds are drawn over the square window. The single bed is pushed against the wall in the corner, there is a desk and a chair facing the window, a wardrobe, a washstand with a gleaming white basin jutting upwards, square-shaped like a new tooth just pushed through. At least it is clean. I look down at the carpet which is brown and sort of crispy.

I shrug at Oliver. He nods and takes me through to the kitchen.

'You'll be sharing with three others, two nurses and a doctor. The girl that was here before you had no complaints, she said they were all clean, quiet, friendly enough.'

'Sure.'

The kitchen is big, with a dining table and four chairs. The windows look out on to the main road and a row of grand, expensive houses opposite. I open a cupboard near the stove, it's a mistake, infinity of Tupperware rains down, lidless, mismatched, spaghetti-stained, the smell of spices scrubbed with soap. I begin to scoop them up as Oliver stands watching me. He doesn't tut but he looks at his watch.

'I'm sorry,' I say. 'The room is great, can I move in on Friday?'

I straighten up with a stack of containers. He scribbles something down.

'Sure,' he says, 'will you come by the office on Friday morning? We'll set up your payments and give you the keys. I've got to go now, are you okay to show yourself out?' He's already moving down the corridor as I call out my thanks and the door closes and I'm left picking up the mess I made.

There are crusts of oil and dust, grains of rice and a frozen now unfrozen pea, clinging to the corners of the cupboards on the floor. The floor is linoleum, cheap and spongy, but easy to clean. I hear a door opening, footsteps in the corridor. I stand up and I'm surprised to see Jennifer standing in the doorway, wrapped in a white bathrobe, hair-towel turban and pink slippers shaped like unicorns. She is tiny and childlike, a fluffy cloud of comfort, she beams at me, freshness and rest in her face.

'Are you moving in? Brilliant!' She shuffles over to me and hugs me. I'm conscious that I smell stale, look shitty.

'I just came to see the room, I get the keys on Friday,' I muffle into her shoulder.

'Great! I'm so happy to be sharing with someone I actually like!' She puts her hand over her mouth and whispers, 'These guys are all right but no one ever wants to go for a drink after work or do anything fun. We live in the best city in the world and it's like no one wants to see it, or experience it, they're all just here to work.' She rolls her eyes.

I could do with some fun, I could blow off some steam.

She goes over to the fridge and starts rummaging.

'Have you eaten yet? You want something to eat?'

'Are you sure? I was going to get something at work,' I say.

She pulls out a huge container and lifts the lid and my stomach squeezes at the delicious smell of cold chicken curry. She pours it into a saucepan and heats it on the stove. She takes out a jar of mango pickle from the fridge, twists the cap, scoops out a teaspoonful and jams it in her mouth.

'Sorry, I love this stuff. When you really get to know me you'll realise I am actually pretty disgusting!' She laughs and taps the teaspoon on her teeth. 'Nothing quite like curry for breakfast.'

She tells me she's exhausted and I tell her she looks so fresh, how jealous I am that she looks so good and that the nights are killing me.

'Matron has been taking a lot of stick recently for how bad the shifts have been. But she's stuck, what can she do? Tonight is an extra shift for me, I'm helping her out because there's no one there to take charge.'

I nod and tell her that I don't mind the random shifts but it's hard at the moment because I'm not sleeping.

'I feel like I'm losing my mind, Jen. I'm seeing things – messed-up things – not just in my sleep but on the ward.'

She's at the sink washing up, she turns to look at me and says, 'But we all see things on the ward. Especially after a death. I'm forever jumping at shadows, I always see ghosts. Think I see ghosts but they're not really there. Tired eyes and dark corners, sleeping silence, it doesn't take much. We're all wound up, you're not going crazy. We're all just a bit stressed and sad after Danny. Dr Lucas is holding a debrief tomorrow morning, we should hang around for it after handover. It will help.'

But I was seeing things before Danny died.

These visions are in me, they are my veins, they are my heartstrings. They stitch me together, running black stitches. There is blackness in my peripheral vision. She's here now, standing behind me, she cloaks me in her sadness. I put my head down on the table. The domestic sounds of splashing water in the sink, the light clatter of cutlery soothes me, I drift off. Fingers caress the back of my neck, cool fingers, wrinkled from washing dishes. But when I wake, Jennifer is at the counter eating a chocolate biscuit and the fingers still touch and my flesh creeps. I rub the back of my neck, scratching the spectral itch.

'One more shift to go, you can do it. This time tomorrow, you'll be on the train home to your family. Your mother needs to give you a good feed.'

'My mother is great, but not the best cook, we eat plainly at home.'

She snorts with laughter when I tell her I tried my first olive when I was twenty-one and laughs with a rolling belly when I tell her my mother thought avocado was a tasteful colour for a bathroom suite. We laugh together.

We walk into work smiling and chatting. Jennifer tells me about her slight crush on Amir and I remind her of his wife who works in the intensive care unit and she blushes, red roses bloom, her cheeks balloon out, shining red-lit beacons. I look at her and I am so grateful for her easiness, her kindness. I feel okay for now with a friend close by.

It's Not So Easy Saying Goodbye

Tracy is at the nurses' station when we get to the ward. She looks so small bundled in a big coat. Her lips tremble when she sees us, we both put our arms around her and hold her together.

'Thank you for everything you did for me and Danny. I've brought you chocolates. Make sure Rudy doesn't eat them all.' She is crying softly. 'I don't know what I'm going to do now, without my baby.'

Jennifer looks at me over the top of Tracy's head. Her eyes are full of tears. So I say, 'You're not without him, Tracy, he's still a part of you. You're still his mum.'

She nods and sinks into us.

But these are not the words I want to say. I want to tell her that I loved Danny too, that I see his little body in the cot in the empty room. That the alarm goes off and I think she is there calling me. That I would have given my heart, my lungs, my blood if it meant he could be saved.

Jennifer lets go first and wipes her eyes. I let go.

'Will I see you again?' asks Tracy, her eyes wide and pleading. She holds on to my arm.

No is the answer but I don't say anything. Jennifer jumps in and says, 'You'll see me and Dr Lucas and maybe Wilf. We'll be coming to the funeral and we can say goodbye properly then.'

She nods and sniffs and smiles. 'I'd better go, my mum and dad are waiting for me in the car.'

'Goodbye, take care of yourself,' we say.

She leaves. The door swings shut behind her but through the long pane of glass I can see her walking slowly down the corridor. She leaves with empty arms.

It's as Easy as Falling Asleep

The night flies. We fly with it. We are kept busy by all the crying babies. Jennifer is a blur of dark blue I barely see. I try to avoid Wilf but he is stuck with us, seeing the sickest patients and scribbling prescriptions. I don't know what to say to him, I am embarrassed.

I hide in the treatment room, tangling myself up in long lines of antibiotics and fluids. He comes in to give me a drug chart and laughs when he sees the knot I am in. He helps me untangle the lines and then takes my gloved hand and twirls me. I can't help but laugh at his awkward sweetness. And at the right moment, Amir comes in and loads up a tray of medications. Wilf disappears as I help Amir with the drugs. I check his and he checks mine, we correct each other's mistakes.

Florence is awake and vomiting, sleeping and vomiting. Her mother rings the nurse call bell like churches on Sunday morning. When I go to Florence's room, her mother hugs me.

'I'm glad we have you tonight, Laura, it has been an awful day.'

I'm sad to hear it, but glad to be wanted. She has stored up her anxieties of the day and gifts them to me, unwraps them for me, lays them across my shoulders and then lays down in the bed with her daughter, stroking her little bald head. She tells me in whispers that thankfully it's just a mild infection, but Dr Lucas isn't taking any chances and the antibiotics are helping already, the sickness is just a side effect. I nod, but I'm not so sure. I check Florence's temperature and make a mental note to check it again in half an hour. I'll ask Wilf to review her, just to be sure. Before I leave the room, her mother asks me to pray with her, she has grabbed my hand, so I say of course and close my eyes tightly. I am on the verge of tears but I'm not sure why.

No time for tears. No time for tea. Time to see my Buddy.

He has been settled and sleeping until now. Now he is stirring and starving. I sit in the chair, balancing baby in one arm as I spread the blanket across my lap. I unclip the name badge and fob watch from my breast and tuck them in the pocket so that he can nestle against me. I am terrified that his skin will get scratched or marked by the metal of the watch, or a corner of the plastic badge. I bring him into my lap and wrap the blanket around him. Pink blotches creep over his cheeks and in the creases of his mouth as he starts to cry, the cry starts as a little crackle in the back of his throat. I try to catch the cry and take it from him as I grab the bottle of formula from the table in reach, I flick a few drops of milk on my arm to test the temperature and bring the teat to his lips. When his mouth opens wide to scream, I press the teat gently on his tongue, he licks blindly, head jerking wildly until he finds the fold, his mouth closes and he sucks greedily. The blotches recede, his skin smooths out, eyes open, all fluttering lashes and wide wet pupils. Peace and pleasure radiate from his little face. I stroke his velvet cheek. His chubby fist grasps my hand as I hold the weight of the bottle. He sucks hard, bubbles whizz to the top of the milk and pop against the plastic. I slowly pull the bottle away from his lips, he grips the teat with his gums, then yields as I tilt him up on to my knee. He gasps as I bring his body upright, I tuck my hand under his chin and he burps with ease. He settles back for seconds.

He is hot in my arms. I loosen the blanket around him. His suck has slowed down and he is drinking steadily. I dab away the little dribbles of milk that escape from his lips. I glance over at Dad who is quietly snoring in the bed. The TV glows but is muted, there is a long advert for an exercise video playing. There is a soft hum and whir from the monitor and muffled sound of bleeping from the room next door. I'm glad Dad didn't wake up, I selfishly wanted a quiet moment and a sit-down.

I gently run my fingers over Buddy's head, his hair is soft and cottony. He drifts in and out of sleep, his sucking slows, nearly stops, and then he pops like a bubble, wakes up to drink some more, tries to push against the heavy dreams that draw his eyelids closed. It is all too much for him in the end. His head rolls back and he surrenders the bottle in favour of sweet sleep. With my finger I touch the tip of his chin. His pink mouth still sucks a bottle in his dreams.

He smells sweet and sour and soapy. I raise him higher in my lap. His neck is nestled into the crook of my arm. I rock him and I feel like singing. In this holding, I am healing, he is dreaming and I feel content. This is where I'm supposed to be. This is why I'm here. A sick baby on his way to being well. On his way to being well because of surgery, medication, holding, sleeping, something. I wish I knew which one it was because then we could do more. Save more babies. Sometimes none of it works. I think about this all of the time.

I cradle the baby. I touch his arm, feel the flesh through the thin vest he is wearing. The vest is speckled with milk and splattered with other unknown stains. I will change him before I put him back in his cot but I want to sit here a while longer. I place my hand on his belly, feel it full, rising and falling.

In sleep he abandons his limbs. He is weighty and weightless at the same time. The warmth of his flesh melds with mine, no distinguishable start to him or end to me, we are the same, we are rolling together, slowly swaying in a hypnotic, sleepy trance.

I picture the little puddle of milk inside him, rippling rings on the surface, starting small in the centre of his stomach with a gurgle and then growing outwards, widening circles. I step into the circle with him in my arms, the air presses against me, heavy, thick and warm like wading through melted marshmallow and it is hard to walk with marshmallow on your shoes.

You come to pick me up from work in your car. Excitement tingles through me when I see you, leaning over the steering wheel, grinning at me through the windscreen.

We kiss like the world is ending because it is.

You drive fast and I laugh and shriek with bumps and sharp corners. We know these roads like we know our own skin. You drive with one hand loosely on the steering wheel, one hand shifting between the gear stick and my knee. I turn on the radio and settle on a song I can sing too. You grin when I hit a high note. I reach to touch your cheek. A song from childhood plays. We both say at the same time it reminds us of our fathers.

These are the roads my father drove, pointing out pheasants, falling stone walls, shooting ranges. I would stare up at the clouds moving with us through the valley. My father would point with one long finger, close one eye like a sniper and I would shout POP. We were cloud bursting. And it rained, it rained, it rained.

In the daytime we rush through green, always green forests. In the night-time we race past the aching white skeletons of trees wrapped in wreaths of grey leaves, ragged wood with knotweed faces, mouths opening coldly. The headlights flash and I glimpse her hanging in the darkness, floating in patches of mist. Perhaps she has always been with me.

With you I am not scared of her, not scared of anything. This is how we used to feel. Fearlessly speeding around the bends, with the windows rolled down, with my hair blowing in the wind. Driving through the long summer nights, the dream days, dream haze, I remember nothing but laughing, the warmth of your touch, this is the happiest I have ever been in my whole life. But the touch has turned cold, there is ice in your fingers – but these are not your fingers and the hand is on my shoulder and not on my knee and it is not tenderly touching, it is sharply pinching. Slow down, slow down, we are going too fast. Her fingers tighten on my shoulder, the brakes are not screeching but she is screaming. You slam on the brakes but it is too late.

I know what is happening but it is too late. I know what has happened.

I look down, past my empty lap, to the floor. I see the little arms and the little legs splayed. The broken body, the broken bones, white as milk, soft as chalk.

Acknowledgements

Thank you to Alexandra Pringle, Todd McEwan and Lucy Ellmann for seeing what I can't see, for your encouragement and belief in me. Thank you to Allegra Le Fanu for your time, hard work and ability to frame my writing articulately and beautifully. Thank you to everyone at Bloomsbury for gathering up my dreams and binding them into reality.

I would like to thank my wonderful agent Niki Chang, I am so grateful that we found each other. Your dedication, ambition and work ethic is inspirational. Thank you for just being there.

Thank you to my family for their love and support, always. Thank you to my mother Christine for inspiring me to become a nurse and for being endlessly caring and compassionate.

Thank you to Tom for holding me when I am too exhausted to stand up any longer, for easing my doubtful mind, for spending each day with me.

Anna, Tim, Harry and Hugo, I am thankful for your enthusiasm, openness and friendship. I remain in awe of your talent.

The list of colleagues and friends I have worked with throughout my nursing career is long, but I would like to thank the Lauras, Ellas, Jennifers, Rachels, Hollys, Melitas and MJs for working alongside me, giving time, kindness and care in often challenging circumstances. I feel blessed to work with you.

I would like to acknowledge the musical genius of The National, Rufus Wainwright, Joanna Newsom, Solange, La Dispute and Fleetwood Mac whose music carries me into the light and enables me to write boldly and truthfully.

A Note on the Type

The text of this book is set in Bembo, which was first used in 1495 by the Venetian printer Aldus Manutius for Cardinal Bembo's *De Aetna*. The original types were cut for Manutius by Francesco Griffo. Bembo was one of the types used by Claude Garamond (1480–1561) as a model for his Romain de l'Université, and so it was a forerunner of what became the standard European type for the following two centuries. Its modern form follows the original types and was designed for Monotype in 1929.